SEEDS OF WAR

BOOK 1

INVASION

A Semper Fi Press Book

A Semper Fi Press Book

ISBN-13: 978-1-945743-25-2
ISBN-10: 1-945743-25-5

Printed in the United States of America

Cover by Jesh Snow

<u>DEDICATION</u>

To the SMOFs and fans who created

the San Juan, Puerto Rico NASFiC
and the Helsinki, Finland WorldCon.

Your tireless efforts produced many wonderful
outcomes, including two authors from different
worlds coming together in the unlikely partnership
that resulted in this book.

Thank you.

SEEDS OF WAR
Book I: Invasion

Part I: Dreams and Response

"General, Second Battalion's lines are crumbling. What are your orders?"

Colby looked up from his console as he tried to comprehend what the red-faced colonel was asking.

Second Battalion's lines were crumbling? Which second battalion, and how the hell could that happen?

The fact that one of his units was engaged was a complete surprise to him. The division was only deployed as a show of force, not to kick off a war.

"General, what now?" the colonel insisted.

Colby didn't even recognize the colonel, but he cut the connection with his boss, the force commander, with whom he'd been discussing the political situation, and turned back to his console. A moment ago, the display had been clear, but now, red alarm stars were pulsing over the entire front. A swarm of red arrows were pushing through the blue unit symbols of his Marines. As he watched, Second Battalion, Fifth Marines disintegrated, down to 20 percent.

"General!" the colonel insisted once again.

Colby shook his head. He didn't have an operations order for this. His G3 would have 50 such plans in the files for any contingency, but Colby wasn't prepared for this. He looked around the Command Post, but his Three wasn't there. Twenty faces looked to him for orders.

Hell, I'm Lieutenant General Colby Merritt Edson, Republic Marines, and this is what I'm trained for.

"What's the status on the arty?" he asked, transitioning into command mode.

"Two heavy and one light battery are in place, the mobile and one light are displacing," a major replied.

Colby powered up the terrain model in the middle of the CP, instructed his AI to overlay the battle onto it, and said, "Give me sheath volleys, here, here, and here. It's too late for Two-Five, but maybe we can stem the tide and give us a moment to dig in."

A heavy battery, with its 24 tubes of 225mm shells, could create a virtual wall of steel, covering 1200 meters of front.

"What's the status on the Navy? What do we have in orbit? Can we get support?"

"That's a negative, General," a lieutenant commander said. "The ship's inner system drive is down."

"Tell the captain that he'd better get that drive up and running. We need those guns now!" he shouted.

Damned piece-of-shit Navy! Never there when we need them.

That wasn't a fair accusation, he knew. He had Academy classmates in the Navy, and they were plagued by the same lack of replacement and spare parts as the Corps was, and half of the parts they did receive were faulty.

No use bitching about it now. If no naval guns, then it's got to be air.

"Air Officer," he shouted, "what do we have on station?

"Nothing on station, sir," a lieutenant colonel said.

Colby had to take two deep breaths or he was going to go off on the woman. "And why the hell not?"

"Your orders, General. You said not to waste flight hours. You said you didn't want to break the aircraft."

Colby didn't remember giving any such orders, although that had become standard practice. Air capability had become a balancing act between pilot hours and airframe hours. The pilots needed them to remain proficient, and the planes needed limited hours so the crews could keep them airworthy.

"What can we get in the air, then?"

"Two Specters and a Wraith, sir."

"Out of eighteen craft in the squadron? Hell, I'm going to have to fire me a squadron commander. Get those three in the air, now, priority of fire to. . ." he paused, taking a look at the developing battle on the terrain model. "Priority of fire for the Specters to Fifth Marines, the Wraith in general support."

"Who exactly is attacking us?" he asked. "Two?"

Colonel Juan French, his G2, said, "The Defenders of Truth, General."

"What? The DOT?"

That didn't make any sense at all. The DOT was all talk and bluster. They'd never shown the will nor the capability to launch a military offensive.

"Roger that, sir. It's them."

"If they want to play with the big boys, we'll crush them," he muttered.

He took a moment to digest the battle. Amateurs or not, they had pushed right through the division's lines. Even if the Marines had not expected an offensive, there was no way they should have been able to prosecute their assault so well.

"Who's got Seventh Marines," he asked, confused as to why he didn't know such a simple fact.

"Colonel Harris Bellemy-Mohamed," the red-faced colonel said.

Harris? My classmate? How did that slip my mind? he wondered before pushing the thought aside.

He opened up the comms on a Person-to-Person line and passed, "Colonel, this is General Edson. The DOT is sweeping through Fifth Marines. I need you to pull back, then create a hasty line of defense along the ridge running from zero-three-three-eight to zero-three-four-five. I'll give you air and arty support, but you need to move it now. You've got forty mikes to get into position."

"Uh, Colby, I'm not so sure we can do that. We're having problems with our ammo. I think you gave us a bad shipment."

"I what?" he asked astounded.

"You're the Commanding General of the Marine Corps Logistic Command, so yeah, I put in on your shoulders."

"What the. . . ? Logistic Command?" he asked, going apoplectic. "I'm your fucking division commander, and I'm ordering you to move, now!"

"Get us good ammo, and maybe we will. I'm not going to fight without it, Colby." The colonel's smug tone underscored addressing him as "Colby" and not "General."

Colby stood up in his chair, barely keeping the volcano inside of him from erupting. Classmate or not, this. . . this refusal to follow orders was completely unsat.

"I'm going to court martial his ass as soon as this is over. He'll rot in the brig!"

No wonder he never got his star, the piece of shit. How did he even make O6?

He forced the colonel out of his mind. He had an entire division under his command, and he didn't need the Seventh Marines to crush the DOT. Maybe if he slid Ninth Marines to the north. . .

"General, one of the Specters just went down," the air officer told him.

"The DOT have Gen Six Anti-air? Since when?"

"It wasn't shot down. One of the ion thrusters fell off," she told him in the same calm and collected voice as if telling him his hover back at home needed a new rearview cam.

"It. . . it fell off?" he said, wondering to what level of hell he'd been sent.

"That's what the pilot said."

An explosion shook the CP, dust rising from the ground to obscure the terrain model. Captain Jersey Rialto, his long-time aide, rushed in and took him by the arm.

"We've got to get you out of here," the captain shouted, pulling him towards the hatch. "I've got a Hydra ready for you."

"Wait, Jersey," he shouted, resisting the burly captain's pull.

The dust was settling enough so he could see the terrain model. Seventh Marines was falling apart before his eyes, blue lights winking out as the running count of Marine KIAs kept rising. Ninth was in contact, and as he watched, the Wraith was shot out of the sky. Unbelievably in less than five minutes, a Marine division had been rendered combat ineffective. It was categorically impossible, but there it was right in front of his eyes.

"Sir, the Hydra won't wait forever," Captain Rialto said.

"Tell the pilot to take off," he told his aide. "I'm staying."

Captain Rialto hesitated, and for a moment Colby thought his aide would bodily pick him up and load him on the shuttle, but then the young man nodded and stepped aside.

A series of snaps filled the CP, making everyone duck, including Colby. He looked up, and a line of holes stitched the walls of the CP. They'd taken fire. He turned back to the terrain model, and where a moment ago there were no DOT forces within five klicks of the CP, now they were surrounded. The rifle company assigned to CP security was in a fight for their lives, and they were losing that fight.

Generals didn't fight battles, they planned them. That was the SOP, at least. But Colby was a warrior at heart, and there really wasn't any option left to him.

"You, prepare a report back to Force, let them know what's happened. Everyone else, suit up! We're going to fight!"

There was a loud "Ooh-rah!" as Marines and sailors rushed to the line of battlesuits in their cradles. Captain Rialto beat Colby to his suit and had started powering it up for him. Colby jumped up and grabbed the support bar, twisting his body like a pro as he slipped into the suit.

"Ready?" the captain asked.

"Hit it."

A moment later, the suit surged to life, straightening and coming back erect. Lights flashed as systems came online. Colby inhaled deeply. He'd had a long career, both as an enlisted Marine and officer, and he'd spent much of that time in his combat armor. There was a smell, a cross between a locker room and a garage, that both got his blood pumping and made him feel at home.

Colby had no idea how the DOT was defeating Marines, and he didn't have much of a hope that any of them would survive, but if he was going to go out, he couldn't think of a better way to do it, fighting with his fellow Marines.

As his suit gave a final confirmation, Colby reverted to company commander mode, quickly outlining a basic plan which the colonels, sergeants major, and other senior officers and enlisted acknowledged, Colonel French became a platoon commander. Sergeant Major Lammi, who'd been his sergeant major when he was a recruit all those years ago, became his first sergeant, as the entire CP staff thundered to the sound of gunfire.

"Get some!" he shouted, filled with elation.

He charged forward, seeking targets as the Marines around him opened fire. Two DOT fighters hesitated as they saw him bear down on them. Their bright red T-shirts emblazoned with the insipid logo of a hand holding a star made them easy targets. The younger one, a slender, pock-marked youth who couldn't have been twenty, raised his old rifle.

Youth or not, he was the enemy, and Colby raised his own 18mm chattergun to cut him down. The young man fired, his round pinging harmlessly off Colby's chest carapace.

You shouldn't have come, son, he thought, as the sights of his chattergun locked on the boy's center of mass.

Colby triggered the gun, but instead of a whine of 20 rounds being fired, there was a clunk. He tried to fire again, but nothing happened. In front of him, the look of terror on the young man's face disappeared to be replaced by one of surprise first, then satisfaction. His buddy had already fled, but he started walking forward.

Colby didn't understand why his gun hadn't fired, but the boy was playing with fire. Not only was Colby experienced in combat and fighting, but he was in a battlesuit, armor that massed 540kg empty. He'd crush the boy with one blow of the fist.

He stepped forward to meet the boy, but the suit remained motionless. It would not respond to his movements. Colby checked the readouts, and 18 of the 23 were red. His suit had crashed hard, and it wasn't going to be moving again without a complete overhaul.

Colby didn't understand how a suit could fail like that, but he couldn't just sit there, spam in a can. He hit the emergency molt. . . and hit it again when nothing happened. The bottom light, which he'd never noticed before, was clearly marked "Molt," and it flashed red.

The faceplate of his armor was clear, and even without his combat display being projected on it, he could see the battle unfolding, at least what was in view. Over the young man's shoulder, he saw Captain Rialto rushing toward him. Colby allowed himself a small exhalation of relief before his aide exploded in a huge ball of fire.

"No!" he shouted, unable to believe that Jersey was gone.

To his right, he caught sight of Colonel French, on his back, with three DOT fighters prying at him with what looked like crowbars. French's arms waved feebly until one of the fighters managed to push his crowbar right through the colonel's torso despite the armor.

This cannot be happening. It's impossible!

And then the young man was standing in front of him, his pimply face up against Colby's faceplate as he tried to peer inside. He held up a hand beside his face as if trying to cut down the glare. After a moment, he shrugged, and with a wicked smile, reached into his cargo pocket and brought out a small GT-3 grenade.

'Oh, shit," Colby said, his heart jumping to his throat.

The GT-3 grenade burned rather than exploded, and at 2300 degrees Celsius, Colby's combat armor wouldn't even slow it down.

The young man held the grenade up in front of his faceplate, making sure Colby could see it. He pointed to it with his free hand and opened it suddenly, then dropped the open hand slowly, mimicking a detonation and it burning down through his armor.

He's enjoying this, the piece of shit. Just get it over with.

The man placed the grenade on Colby's shoulder, steadied it, then took half a step back. Colby tried to move, hoping to knock it off, but his suit remained stubbornly frozen. His tormentor cautiously reached over and set the detonator before hopping back five meters. Colby could just see the grenade sitting there, but he chose to focus on the young man instead, vowing to put on a brave face.

A small sun erupted on his shoulder, blinding him, and a moment later, an unbearable blast of heat engulfed him.

"NO. . .

. . ." he shouted, kicking out his leg. Duke yelped in protest as she fell to the floor.

It took a moment for Colby to come to his senses, his heart pounding as if to burst through his chest.

"Sorry, Duke," he muttered as he sat up in the dark.

Colby's dreams haunted him. They all had a similar theme. Sometimes he was a sergeant, sometimes a captain, sometimes a general, but he was always in a position of authority, and the situation was always dire. He never actually knew what was going on, in the same way he'd often dreamt as a kid that he had a test for a subject he hadn't studied. In these dreams, his Marines looked to him for answers, answers he didn't have. Whatever he could devise never worked, not necessarily because of his plan, but because equipment always failed.

"Sergeant Major Lammi, glad you could make an appearance," he muttered.

He often dreamt of people he'd known as a Marine or as a child, but this was the first time his boot camp sergeant major had been in one of his dreams. Heck, he hadn't thought of the man for decades.

The clock on his nightstand flashed a subdued blue 0423. He considered trying to go back to sleep but knew better. Once his nightmare woke him up, sleep tended to escape him. With a sigh, he rolled his feet out of bed as Duke crept back up and lay beside him. She gave two whumps of her tail and was fast asleep again.

"That's right girl, it's easy for you."

The long-haired, ruddy gold dog had been a bedraggled mess when he arrived and took possession of the farm. Four baths and a bar of soap later, she emerged as a rather pretty dog in the golden retriever vein.

He got out of bed, took care of his toiletries, then sat at the battered desk he'd scrounged from a neighboring farm when he'd first arrived. He pulled up his account. As usual, the inbox was pretty empty. There was a message from a former Marine who'd been lance corporal in the battalion he'd commanded some 17 years prior. The lance corporal was inviting him to his wedding. Colby didn't remember the man, but if the former Marine thought enough to invite him, he deserved a response. The wedding was on Ceylon 2, so he couldn't really go, but he wrote a congratulatory message with what he hoped were enough semper fi platitudes to fill the bill.

He pulled up the latest crop prices, but that somehow got sidetracked to a story on ancient Phoenician agriculture, and that led to the god Ba'al, which led to Norse gods which led to. . .

suffice it to say that two hours later, he was still at his console and hadn't yet learned the day's price for pyro berries.

He needed to cut the deep dive into trivia, so he got up to make a cup of coffee. As soon as he opened the cupboard, Duke came bounding out of the bed, begging eyes fixed on him. He couldn't resist a pretty female, so he poured her a bowl of kibble, which she wolfed down, tail wagging. She looked back up at him hopefully, but when he didn't pour her more, she wandered over to the couch and plopped herself down on it.

Time to get to work, he told himself as he took his coffee back to the desk. He pulled up the prices, which had jumped higher from the day before. Next, he checked the maintenance schedule, created after his ag AI had performed its morning analysis. As usual, there was nothing that had to be fixed. His farm pretty much took care of itself, and the equipment was reliable.

Not like in the military, he thought, going back to his dream, which stubbornly refused to fade away.

Not that the military was as bad as in his dream—not *quite* as bad, that is. But still, with his last command, maintenance and parts acquisition had been his prime focus.

Lost in the past, he stared at his readouts for a full minute before his mind returned to the task at hand. He shook his head once, then focused on the data dump. After nine months, the complex algorithms were only beginning to make sense to him. Not enough, though, for him to make a rational decision. With a sigh, he hit the "Accept," and the day's irrigation plan his AI had recommended went into effect.

He didn't have to review the AI's recommendation, but at least by doing so, he could pretend that he was vital to the process. It still grated on him that he was little more than a caretaker on his own farm. He'd commanded a Marine division in combat, after all, and now he couldn't even make a decision on how much water went to each field. Most of the other farmers on Vasquez, heck, probably throughout human space, let the ag AIs do the work, but Colby prided himself on being a man of action. As usual, he was tempted to override the AI, to adjust what it recommended, but he realized that would only result in a lower yield, and that would be detrimental to the war effort. He may have resigned his commission in disgrace, but he still understood his duty. If this was how he now served the Republic, then he would salute and march on.

He knew he couldn't complain about his situation. He might no longer be on active duty, but life on the farm wasn't so bad. The work wasn't difficult, and as he looked out the window to his fields, there was a sense of accomplishment. His farm provided much needed supplies to both the teeming masses of the megablocks as well as to the armed forces. A man could take pride in that, should take pride. And yet. . . he felt a hole in his life. Transitioning from being the commanding general of the Marine Corps Logistics Command to being alone on his farm had been an adjustment, one he hadn't yet completed.

He turned around, his eyes drawn to his "I Love Me" wall, where holos, flat pics, and plaques hung, all he had left to commemorate his time in the Corps. They covered the entire back wall of his small one-room farmhouse. I Love Me walls were supposed to be celebrations of a military man's career, but Colby's reminded him of his failure, it reminded him of what could have been. He'd been tempted to take everything down, to pack the items in boxes and store them in his vault, but he'd kept the wall up. Taking his holos and plaques down would be giving in to Vice Minister Greenstein, of ceding the field of battle to a man even pond scum would look down upon. Colby had never fled any field of battle, and he wasn't about to start now. Instead, he kept the mementos of his life hung on the wall as he lived alone on a backwards planet in the far reaches of human space.

He wasn't completely alone on the farm, however. "Let's go take a look at the morning harvest, Duke," he said to the old dog that he'd inherited when he'd taken over the place.

Duke wagged her tail twice, but didn't get up from where she was laying on the couch. As a career Marine, Colby had never owned a pet, and it had taken him awhile to realize that the dog he'd named "Duke" was a she, not a he. He never bothered to change her name.

"Come on, Duke. I mean it."

Marines used to jump at his slightest whim, but this old dog was a different story. There was an ancient saying about letting sleeping dogs lie, but he was a general, dammit, and besides, she was not technically asleep. He walked over to the couch and gently pushed on her butt until she gave in to the inevitable and slid off. Once down, she looked up at him with hopeful eyes.

"No. You had breakfast already."

At "breakfast," her tail started wagging in earnest.

Ah, hell, he thought, feeling like a patsy as he went to the cupboard and took out two Happy Pooch doggie treats to give to her. He waited while she gulped them down without so much as a single chew, then with her on his heels, walked out of the door and onto his porch.

He took a deep breath, filling his lungs. Vasquez might be a backwater planet on the edge of human space, but the air was clean and brisk, something that all the scrubbers back on the more densely populated worlds of the Republic couldn't duplicate. The terraformers had done an amazing job on the planet, eradicating all traces of the native vegetation—everything from ancient forests of spike trees to inhospitable plains of poisonous thorn grass—to make it into a human paradise. Crops grew as if on steroids and without the pests and diseases that plagued other worlds.

There was still a trace of morning dew on the grass, and he made a show of kneeling to touch it. "Another twenty minutes, Duke, and the harvesters can start."

The AI had determined that the lowest 20 hectares of pyro berries were ready for harvest. The genetically modified berries were calorie-dense food at 18 kwH/kg. A year ago, Colby didn't know a watt-hour per kilogram from a hole-in-the-ground. Now, he knew that 18 kwH/kg was damned good. By midmorning, he'd have 400 tons of the berries harvested and loaded into an automated cargo pod bound for the port where they'd be shot into space to a processing station on New Mars on the other side of a wormhole, to be put into energy bars or jolt-shakes to feed Marines and sailors—at least that was who he hoped would consume them. His berries could just as easily—and more probably—be made into food for the civilian masses, but he chose to assume for the tenuous connection to his previous military life.

Colby could return to the house, pop a holo in the player, and waste away the morning on the couch, but that wasn't in him. Instead, followed by Duke, he wandered down a meticulously manicured path to the field where the berries were to be harvested. It wasn't that he maintained the path. No non-commercial vegetation had been allowed to be established on Vasquez, so weeds and other superfluous plants were non-existent.

Colby's three-month old HRI-30 harvester hadn't yet begun by the time the two of them arrived. The micro-sensors were reading the moisture content on the berries, and at exactly the right moment, the harvester would begin its task. Colby knelt beside one of the plants at the outer edge of the field, picked a berry, and again made a show of rolling it between his fingers though Duke couldn't have been less interested. He popped it into his mouth, bit, and almost as quickly spit it back out, grimacing at the rotten-corpse taste. It still amazed him that the berries tasted so nasty, yet could be transformed into delicious jolt-shakes and hundreds of other delectable and nearly addictive snacks.

"Yep, Duke, they're ready," he said as the dog lay down, put her head on her crossed front paws, and went to sleep.

With a whir, the squat "Henry" harvester started into motion. Colby was still fascinated at how the meter-wide bot could advance down the field, looking like it was going to crush his plants, yet leave each one standing undamaged, but minus its crop. The type of plant didn't seem to matter. Whether that was Wasabia japonica, pyro berries, corn, or anything else on his farm, the same harvester did the job.

Colby blinked up his implant. As a Marine general, he'd had the highest-level implant available to man, and when he'd resigned his commission, it hadn't been military policy to try swap it out for a civilian model. Instead he'd simply undergone a quick procedure to deactivate the secure access function. Now, with the same 500,000-credit implant that would have allowed him to command a division in combat, he pulled up the harvest readouts. The numbers were excellent, both in production and quality of the berries. If the harvest continued with the same results, he'd be in for a quality bonus.

Not that I need it, he told himself. *What am I going to spend it on here?*

Colby had never married. The demands of the service had been too great. He'd dated a few times as a junior officer, but women quickly realized that his dedication was to the Corps, and not to them. Now, on Vasquez, with its extremely sparse population, there wasn't much potential on the horizon. He had a handful of nieces, nephews, and their children, but none had paid much attention to him in the past, so they could go suck on an egg, for all he cared.

"If you outlive me, girl, you're going to be one rich dog."

Duke whumped her tail twice on the dirt, then went back to sleep.

Colby's stomach rumbled.

While he'd fed Duke after waking, not wanting to feel her accusing eyes on him, he hadn't eaten himself, and he wouldn't eat until after his workout. He was still young and fit at 73 Standard Years, but he wouldn't be if he let his body go to hell. He had a good fifty or so more years left to him, and he'd be damned if he'd do that sitting on a couch and simply observing the universe pass him by. Six days a week, he went through his Marine Corps PT program.

"OK, girl, Henry's got this in hand. Let's get back."

Ten minutes later, he was back on his porch in just running shoes and shorts, no shirt. In the

Corps, he'd run in whatever was the official PT gear at the time, and despite keeping up with his Marine grooming regs, he felt a little guilty at this small act of rebellion. He'd even once run stark naked, the ultimate rebel, until he realized that wasn't the most practical way in which to jog. So, now a pair of shocking pink shorts and civilian running shoes were the most obvious manifestation of his rebellion.

"You coming?" he asked Duke as he stretched.

She watched him with what looked to be interest, but he knew she'd just lay on the porch as he ran around the farm, waiting for him to give her a second breakfast while he ate his.

He easily jumped over the four steps leading off the porch and broke into a comfortable lope as he warmed up. As he reached the southeast corner of the farm, down by the winter melon patch, he picked up the pace. Within 500 meters, the sweat was forming and rolling down his chest as the machine of his body started humming. He might not be 25 any longer, but he felt like he was, and he reveled in how easily he ran along the perimeter path.

After eight klicks, he gave a salute to Henry as he ran around the lowest 20 hectares, then sped up as he climbed back up to the house, sprinting the final 200 meters. It didn't look as if

Duke had moved since he'd taken off, but she sat up as he came to a stop, bent over at the waist, hands on his knees, to catch his breath.

"Just give me a moment, girl," he said, chest heaving like bellows.

He grabbed the towel he'd placed on the porch rail and wiped his face. It took a moment, but something hit him as odd. He gave the towel a sniff, and it smelled, well, *green,* if a color could smell. He took another sniff, then looked closely at it. Instead of just Colby-sweat, he could see small specks of something. It wasn't until that moment that he realized that his skin felt different, too. Wiping his hand on his chest, he could feel something rough and almost gritty. It wasn't dirt, he could see as he examined his hand. Whatever it was looked organic to him.

He immediately looked up to the north. One of the old terraforming projectors was in that direction, about 20 klicks away. Vasquez was a Class 1 world, fully terraformed. It shouldn't need any more adjustment to the environment.

Maybe there is something they're doing and I missed the announcement?

From beside him, Duke whined, putting her right paw on his thigh.

"OK, OK, girl, I get the message."

He opened the door and let her in, then stripped and went into the shower. As the water jets scoured his skin, he couldn't help but note the surprisingly large number of specks, or whatever they were, flowing off his body to swirl down the drain.

It was rare for the small residual TF office on the planet to do even minor tweaks, but if they were doing something, that could affect his farm. . . . He'd have to check to find out.

"After chow, though. I'm pretty hungry," he said to himself, and his stomach rumbled again in agreement.

****

Colby let out a satisfied, and completely non-reg, burp as he climbed up on his Number 3 wind turbine, the taste of bacon coming back for a second time. One of the advantages of living on Vasquez was the readily available meat products, not the least being thick, applewood-smoked bacon. Even as a Marine general, most of his protein, and much of his other food, was fabricated in huge food factories, the kind of which the bulk of his crops provided the raw materials. Despite the scientists swearing that their factory-grown slabs of meat could not be distinguished from the real thing, no one believed that. And while Colby only grew crops, there were more than a few ranchers who raised chickens, turkeys, pigs, and cows for the rich and powerful, those men and women at the top of the Republic's corporate and government ladders.

Cost for moving foodstuffs out of the gravity well had come down significantly over the last 30 years, but still, it wasn't cheap. Along with the specialty vegetables (such as Colby's winter melons), meat couldn't be preprocessed at Vasquez' ag station, so the cost to transport it was high. That meant the costs were relatively low on the planet, and he had arrangements with several ranchers to barter winter melons, pomegranates, and densuke melons for beef, pork, and chicken.

He reached above his head and tried to twist the offending vane into place. It didn't' budge. Colby's farm was completely self-reliant for power. Solar panels, four wind turbines, and a methane digester provided for all his energy needs. With the single automated hover rail that took his products to the port and delivered what he needed, Colby rarely had to leave the farm let alone interact with another human being.

It looked like he would be having a guest over to the farm, however. Number 3 was only producing at 94 percent. That wouldn't affect his operations, but 51 years in the military had ingrained in him to be prepared for any eventuality. If other systems went down, then that missing six percent from Number 3 would be felt.

The problem was that while the turbine's analytics pinpointed the issue, it could not correct the physical problem, and none of Colby's tugging was having any effect. He'd have to put in a service call to get one of the techs out to fix it. With four techs on the entire planet (and only one on the continent), that might take a while.

Admitting defeat, he climbed down off the structure, placing the request through his implant. He received an immediate response, and as he expected, an appointment was scheduled in four weeks time.

"Come on, Duke, let's get back to the house," he said.

To his surprise, Duke seemed more interested in something by the hop-beans, another high-caloric base crop for the factories.

"Let's go girl. Lunch!"

Instead, Duke barked, then pawed at something. Curious, Colby knelt beside the dog, wondering what had gotten her worked up. On his home planet of Tiergarten Delta, rabbits and other small animals had been released into the wild, so there were things for a dog to chase. But this was Vasquez. There weren't animals on the planet that had no commercial value. Earthworms, bees, and livestock, yes. Rabbits or other small mammals that could eat the precious crops, no.

But it wasn't a mammal that had caught Duke's attention. To his surprise, Colby saw several small plant-like. . . *things*. . . under the broad leaves of the hop-beans. He used the term "plant-like" because while they looked like vegetation of some sort, they were not anything he'd seen before. Naturally meticulous and with time on his hands, Colby had studied every crop and plant that had been introduced on the planet. Whatever these were, they were not on the list.

It was possible that these were some sort of nitrogen-fixing genmod that was being introduced, but when Colby had queried the net for info right after breakfast, he'd come up blank. For a Class 1 world to have something else introduced, there would have been tons of forums and debate, days and days of documentation and recordings to wade through. It was inconceivable that the planet's inhabitants would not have been part of the process. Things like this, usually fueled by corporate greed or governmental experiments, had occurred before, almost always with disastrous results.

And whatever the small, five-centimeter-tall things were, they didn't look like normal plants. They had a central stalk, a leafy, compact crown, and what looked like thick, ropy roots splayed under them. Weirder still, they seemed oriented to Duke and him, as if they were watching them.

He slowly moved to his right, and while he couldn't be sure, it seemed like they were following him.

Come on, Colby, *get ahold of yourself. You've been alone too long. It's bad enough that you talk to Duke like she's human, but this. . . ?*

Whatever the things were, they bothered him. Plants, even genmodded plants with who knows what genes spliced into them, didn't grow this fast. If they had, in fact, come from the specks that had landed on him during this run, they were way too big a mere three hours later.

"Let's go, Duke, now!" he said, pulling back on her neck scruff.

He shuddered, then quickly walked back up the path to his vault. He could see more of the plant-things along the way, and he could have sworn that some actually moved off the path as he approached.

But that's impossible, right?

The door whooshed open as he approached. He grabbed a hand-sprayer and he went straight to the rack of cylinders, where 20 were on three offset shelves, tubes sprouting from the tops like crazy Medusas. It took him a moment to find the right one, then by bypassing the main feed tube, he managed to fill his sprayer with RU-22. He gave it a tentative spray, and it emitted a fine mist. The vault's air evac system sucked it up and away into a catch-vent.

Duke had jumped at the mist, but as it didn't seem to hurt her, she poked her nose forward, sniffing the sprayer.

"No, you don't want that," he told her, holding it higher, out of her reach.

All of the RU products were certified safe for animal life, but if it killed plants that easily, Colby wasn't sure it was totally harmless. He grabbed a mask out of the dispenser by the door, put it on, then went forth to do battle.

He didn't have to go all the way to the perimeter fields. Field 2A, which was also a pyro berry field, was in the middle of the eastern sector. He thought he saw movement, so he stopped and crouched down. There, under the bushes, were close to a hundred of the small plants. He held the sprayer forward, close to them, and sprayed. A fine mist coated them and the nearest berry bushes. He hated to sacrifice the half-dozen bushes, but the invading plants gave him the creeps.

Almost immediately, the plants reacted, as if trying to evade the spray. RU-22 worked quickly, but not that quickly. The berry bushes were already wilting as the spray broke down their cellular walls, but the small plants were writhing—actually writhing—as the spray touched them. Colby knew this had to be caused by their cellulose walls contracting unevenly, but it was still disconcerting.

"Well, at least we know it works, huh Duke?"

She barked in response, then pawed at the nearest of the plants. Colby had to jerk the dog back.

The movement ceased, and the small plant bodies started to decompose. Within five minutes, there was nothing left of them, along with the six berry plants that the mist had touched. With a final nod, he stood and went back into the vault.

RU-22 was an amazingly high-tech herbicide. It was designed to break down plant matter and let it seep back into the soil. This was far more efficient and timely, if more expensive, than the ancient method of plowing plants back into the ground. The problem with earlier versions of the herbicide was that it decomposed in a broad spectrum. Winter melon vines were alive for only one fruiting, and if the RU-20, the older version of the herbicide, was used to decompose the melon field drifted to, say his pyro berry field, where the bushes lasted two to three years before yields began to fail, then it would kill the berry bushes as well. Monsanto's solution was to have genetic blockers mixed in with the RU-22 that made it harmless to targeted crops. If he'd targeted the RU-22 in his sprayer for pyro berries, then they wouldn't have died when he'd sprayed the invading plants.

Colby gave the instructions to his ag AI. He wanted his entire farm sprayed, but he didn't want to lose his crops in the process. The AI gave him a price for the operation. He blanched at the cost, knowing it would more than eat up the bonus, and the next ten bonuses, for his bumper crop of pyro berries. He hesitated, then gave the go-ahead. The ag AI started its work, mixing the outgoing RU-22 with the correct genetic blocker for a given field, then sending the spray out. Colby waited for the 30 minutes, afraid the AI would make a mistake and wipe out a field of densuke melons. As usual, however, the AI did its job, and the entire farm was sprayed.

Colby didn't know why he bothered to open the door a crack and peek out first as if checking for an enemy lying in wait. Laughing at his caution, he sauntered down to 2A. The ground was littered with what was left of the tiny plants, the berry plants were untouched. He moved over to 2B, then 2C. It was the same there. He checked each and every field, and by the time he was done, all traces of the invading plant had disappeared into the soil.

Breathing a huge sigh of relief, he turned to go back into the house. He needed to report this to the central office, 3000 klicks away in

Freesome City. He knew he should have kept a sample of the plant, but if they wanted one, all he had to do was go outside his farm and gather a couple.

"Well, girl, I think we did a good job," he said as he plopped down into his kitchen chair. "Nobody, or I guess, *nothing*, is going to invade my farm."

****

Colby lay on his bed, Duke fast asleep and sprawled across his lap. The dog gently snored, a string of drool soaking through the light blanket and onto his thigh.

"At least one of us can sleep, girl."

He hadn't been able to drop off, and he'd ended up binge-watching the final five episodes of "The Beltov Boys." He hated the show. In typical Hollybolly fashion, the writers had just about everything wrong about the military and warfare. Despite this, and despite the fact that he kept pointing out all of the mistakes to the uncaring Duke, he watched every episode. And while he'd deny it until the end of time, he'd had a tear or two form when Anton slipped into death's embrace.

He checked the time. Dawn had just broken, and while he could pull up the next season, his day would begin soon enough. He might as well get a start on things. Carefully sliding Duke off his lap, he got out of bed and dialed up a coffee. Taking the steaming mug, he stood over his display, checking the readouts. As usual, nothing was out of the ordinary. Every reading was within standards.

Colby had lived an eventful life with no less than seven combat tours. Sure, most of his career had not been as exciting, either in desk jobs or in training for combat. But even then, there was always the potential for combat that made the training relevant and gripping. Those days were over, however. Nothing exciting was ever going to happen to him again. Every day, for the rest of his life, he'd check his readouts to see them the same as the day before, the year before, the decade before. Sometimes, he wished that something new would happen, anything to break the monotony.

The gods of war, farms, and just about everything else, are a capricious lot, and as if listening to his thoughts, they chose that moment for one of his motion sensors to go off. Colby's farm was a long way from any of the ranches in the district, too far for a wandering cow to happen by and eye his crops, and this was the first time the alarm had been activated. He tapped the screen a few times, but it remained on. Frowning, he stepped out onto his porch, clad in only his boxers, and looked out towards field 4D at the far eastern edge of his property. He couldn't see anything, not that he expected to. The alarm had to be a bug in the system, which meant his AI could be acting up in more ways than just false motion detector alarms.

That could be catastrophic, and he felt a surge of, well not panic, but concern. For all that he wanted to be in control of the decisions made to run his farm, the thought of actually being forced to make those decisions left him apprehensive.

He looked back through the open door to Duke, still happily asleep, leg twitching as she chased dream rabbits. With a shrug, Colby walked off the porch, barefoot and still in only his underwear, and down one of the paths to 4D. He was sure there wasn't anything there and that this was a glitch, but his military mind wanted to confirm that before he put in a priority call for a tech to check out his AI.

4D was a good 900 meters from the farmhouse, and as he walked, the exertion, coupled with the morning sun, caused him to sweat. Vasquez' sun, a relatively old star as stars go, was heavy in the red-to-blue wavelengths, which made the planet such a good place to grow Earth crops. The standing joke was that a farmer could plant a seed but would have to jump back before the plant sprang out of the ground and hit him in the face.

The morning's rays felt good on his skin. Like all Marines, Colby was extremely self-conscious about letting the sun, any sun, shine on his unprotected skin. On Poulson's World, he'd been terribly burned by the planet's young sun. It hadn't seemed to be generating much heat, but its ultraviolet output had been more than enough to crisp his bare chest and back and land him in the hospital for regeneration for two full weeks. Here on Vasquez, however, the sun put out relatively little ultraviolet light, which was good for plants and human skin alike.

He reached 4D, and as he expected, there wasn't a lone cow on a walkabout eyeing his corn. He was just about to return to the house when something else caught his attention. The plot of land to the east of his was still owned by the government, and it had been planted with sawgrass as a means of erosion control as well as providing ethanol for vehicles. It looked to him as if the sawgrass moved. Except there was no wind at the moment to account for any movement. He took a couple of steps farther down the path, and things came into focus. It wasn't the sawgrass that was moving, but rather something else, something that looked like larger versions of the plant he'd eradicated the night before. About half-a-meter high now, they were definitely moving—slowly to be sure, but moving.

Colby hadn't imagined that the only place the invasive species had landed was on his farm, of course, but seeing as how large the things had grown in the last 15 hours, he was glad he'd killed each of the pests on his property. He wasn't even sure they would harm his crops, but something had his nerves itching much as he used to have before going into battle. He just knew they were bad news.

He squatted right at the edge of his property, peering into the sawgrass at the hundreds, if not thousands, of the plants. He could have sworn that the nearest of them swiveled to him, although if to face him or turn away, he sure couldn't tell.

If these were an invasive species, he really had to report them. He activated the record function on his implant, which pulled the images from his optic nerve. On impulse, he reached over and grabbed one of the plants, expecting to pull its roots out of the ground so he could get a clear recording of it. Two surprising things happened. First, the roots were barely attached into the dirt, if at all. Second, a searing pain shot through his hand and up his arm. He dropped the plant and jumped back. This time, there was no mistake about it; the plant dragged itself back to the sawgrass, its leaves acting as arms.

Colby instinctively started to stomp on the plant, but he pulled back at the last moment as he realized he was still barefoot, almost naked, in fact. His hand was still burning, and suddenly, he felt very vulnerable. He stumbled back five meters, then stood there, watching the plant join the others, then pull itself upright.

I've got to report this.

He tried to connect to Central Ag, but his call wouldn't go through. The channels were jammed. He queued up his recording and left a message, knowing that the call would be received when there was some available bandwidth.

4D was just on the west side of a slight rise on the government land. As Colby stood there, wondering what he should do next, the sun's rays rose enough to illuminate the ground. Almost immediately, there was an increase in activity among the invading plants. He felt an ominous foreboding that something bad was about to happen.

After a few moments of direct sunlight, the plants started walking across the boundary path, their "roots" working like octopus tentacles to move them along. At the edge of the field, the first few plants stopped, leafy arms reaching out to touch the stalks of corn, almost tentatively.

"Got you now, you bastards," he muttered.

He'd sprayed the field with RU-22, which had a two-day period of efficacy. The herbicide would still be more than powerful enough to manage the invasion. A squad of the things was now on the path, but not pushing forward into the corn.

Until they were.

With a sudden surge, the entire mass pushed forward. Leafy green arms reached forward to pull down the corn stalks.

"Oh, no, you don't!" Colby yelled, taking a step forward before common sense again took over.

He was still standing in his underwear, after all, and the things had proven that they had a bite to them. He spun and bolted back up the path, not bothering to watch his field laid to waste. Three minutes later, he burst into the vault.

Evidently, the RU-22 had weakened enough overnight so that the plants could stand up to it. But he'd wiped out the baby plants before, so he was pretty sure he could take care of their bigger siblings. He gave his AI direct orders to initiate the same herbicide sequence as the day before, but starting with 4D. A few moments later, RU-22 was being dispensed.

With a huge sigh of relief, Colby went back to the door and looked down the slope in the direction of the field. He couldn't see much, but he knew the plants would be disintegrating. He wondered if they were screaming tiny plant screams as their plans were foiled. If they were, he didn't care.

It was obvious by now that these were no ordinary plants, but whether the products of some ag lab gone mad or an alien species, he hadn't a clue. Nor did he really care. If they wanted to take his farm, they'd suffer the consequences.

He checked his message, but it was still in the queue. He couldn't be sure, of course, but he had the sinking suspicion that this invasion was not something isolated to the local region.

Colby was not the most sociable neighbor, but on sparsely-populated planets, people helped each other. He gave Gabrielle and Tonsor, his nearest neighbors, a call to warn them. The local nets were not jammed, and the call went through, the visuals opening up to show what had to be their living room in the background. He waited patiently for either of the two to appear. Neither did. He guessed they could be asleep, but farm folk tended to wake up early, and it was already past 7:30 in the morning. If they were out in their vault, their implants would patch them through.

If they were asleep, he had no way to wake them, so he left a message for when they woke up. Hopefully, they'd still have crops by that time. He was about to cut the connection when movement on the screen caught his eye.

"Hey, about time—" he started, before he realized that he hadn't seen Gabrielle or Tonsor.

A plant invader, followed by two more, moved past the pickup. There was a crashing sound, then more of the plants passed into view before the pickup was knocked to the floor, and the connection was cut.

"Holy shit," he said quietly as what he'd seen sunk in.

This was getting serious.

He checked the status of the spraying. 4D and E were completed with five more fields commencing. His entire farm would be covered within 20 minutes. He doubted the plants would be able to reach the farmhouse by then, given what he'd seen.

Suddenly, he felt very vulnerable standing there in his underwear. Ancient warriors might have girded their loins before battle in what was their version of Bryson Mills boxers, but this wasn't then. He bolted for the house and to his closet, pulling out his old Marine Corps camouflaged utilities. He hadn't worn them since his resignation, but they now gave him a sense of purpose. Out came his boots, and as the wraparounds tightened on his feet, it was as if he'd never left. His hand strayed to the armor activation, but that was too much. The RU-22 was killing off the invaders, so it wasn't as if he was going into battle against the Borealis Pact.

"Wake up, Duke," he yelled as he started out the door again. "I said, come, girl," he added while the dog whumped her tail on the bed, but not getting up.

He rolled his eyes and ran to the vault, eager to check the progress. About a third of the farm was sprayed. The motion sensors were still screaming their warnings.

Let them come. As soon as they step on my property, it's mush for them, and I'll grow my crops on their dead bodies.

Satisfied that everything was going according to plan, he tried to call Ag Central one more time, but there was still no connection. Hesitating more than a combat vet should, he tried to get ahold of Gabrielle and Tonsor, but that connection was dead. He knew he should have called them yesterday when he'd first noticed the baby invaders. If he had, they might have had a chance.

He stepped to the doorway and looked out down the slope. It was almost a klick to 4D, so he couldn't be sure, but it looked as if more of his corn was on the ground and the vast swath of sawgrass on the next plot was flattened. The sawgrass made sense. If these things were attacking Earth vegetation, then the sawgrass had no protection. But his fields were being sprayed. They should be stopped in their tracks.

I need to get a closer look.

He may not have the X55 carbine he'd favored while on active duty, but simply being in his utilities gave him a sense of confidence. The plants weren't very large, after all, and his boots made for good stomping if it came to that.

Colby didn't get far. Halfway there, he could see the last of his corn topple to the ground. The RU-22 should be working, but the evidence was right there before his eyes. He turned around and ran back up the hill and into the vault. Checking the readings, he confirmed that the herbicide had indeed been dispensed. He switched the display, and four of his fields were now essentially dead, the numbers showing zero growth.

"Son-of-a-bitch!"

He wasn't sure what to do, so he queried the AI. It recommended increasing the concentration of the RU-22. He hesitated. The first spraying didn't work, so he wasn't sure a second one would, either. But he had nothing else, so he approved the course of action. Within moments, the higher-strength herbicide was being dispensed. Colby watched the readouts, but the damage continued to mount. Eighteen percent of his crops had been destroyed so far, and the damage showed no signs of slowing down. He had to do something.

"Ralph, dispense RU-20 to rows three and four," he ordered the AI, using the name assigned to it when he'd taken over the farm. "Maximum strength."

"RU-20 will destroy all crops," the AI responded. "Please confirm instructions."

No one wanted to employ slash and burn as a strategy, but it was becoming clear that he was fighting a losing battle, and the only thing that made any sense was that somehow the invading plants were being protected by the same genetic blockers that kept his crops safe from the RU-22. It was better to lose half of his crops than all of them. Not just crops, either. The image of the invaders inside Gabrielle and Tonsor's home was gnawing at him. RU-20 was a merciless herbicide, and it would stop the bastards in their tracks.

As the RU-20 made its way down the lines to the fields, Colby tried Ag Central again. This time, he didn't get the full bandwidth error message but rather the "cannot connect" message. He didn't even want to contemplate what that meant, but his military mind wouldn't let it go. The enemy, as he now thought of the plants, had seemingly begun a full-scale invasion. What he didn't know was whether the plants themselves were doing the invading or if they were merely biological weapons employed by another species. Mankind had never yet encountered an intelligent life, but the universe was a vast place, and he was not willing to dismiss any possibility out of hand.

I've got to see what's happening. He opened the door to the vault.

The enemy had cost him half his crops, and that would cripple any hope of profit for the year. He wanted, no, he *needed* to see them destroyed. Once he secured what remained of his farm, he could worry about the rest of the sector.

Standing at the top of the hill, he could see crops disappear as the herbicide did its work. Colby had lost troops in battle. He'd lost friends. Watching his crops being destroyed wasn't the same thing, but it was close. He knew that was a ridiculous sentiment, but he couldn't help the feeling.

Field 3C was the closest of the targeted fields to him, and he watched the hop-beans first shrivel before collapsing onto the dirt. As the beans dropped, they revealed 4C behind it, and hundreds of the enemy plants, each continuing the march forward, seemingly unaffected by Monsanto's best.

"Shit!" he shouted, rushing back into the vault.

"I said maximum strength, Ralph," he told the AI.

"Affirmative. RU-20 was dispensed at the maximum legal strength."

"I don't care about legal or not. I want the max possible."

"Civil Code 4002.3.12 expressly forbids any Class 4 herbicide to be applied above 40 percent concentration without a special use permit."

"I don't give a fuck about Civil Code 4002-whatever. We're under attack. I order you to dispense pure RU-20, no dilution!"

"Your illegal command has been duly noted and forwarded to Ag Central."

"There is no Ag Central anymore, you idiot, Ralph" he yelled.

Colby didn't know if Ag Central still existed or not, but it seemed like a good guess that was the reason he could not connect with them. Not that his AI cared. It was programmed one way, and the end of the universe would not sway the stupid thing. He could scream and shout at it, but that would be beating his head against the wall.

"Dispense RU-20 to all rows," he ordered the AI. "Maximum strength."

"RU-20 will destroy all crops. Please confirm instructions."

You already told me that, he thought, but just before he gave the confirmation, another thought hit him, and he said, "Wait one."

Running back outside, he could see waves of the enemy crossing the now denuded Rows 3 and 4. As they reached Row 2, the invaders started to tear into his crops. Colby was sure that the things had killed his neighbors, and now they were marching towards him. If he cleared the way by destroying his own crops, they would get to him that much sooner.

"You've got to get out of here, Edson," he said aloud.

He wanted to protect his farm, but it wasn't worth his life. He ran to the house where Duke greeted him with a whomp of her tail on the bed.

"Come on, girl. No time for this," he said, snapping a leash around her neck.

Duke resisted, pulling back, but Colby was having none of it. He dragged her to the door and grabbed his bugout bag, a holdover habit from his service days. He turned to give the small house a once over, then pulled the dog outside.

"Pay attention, Duke! Don't give me any shit!"

He started to the west in a slow run, only speeding up when Duke gave into the inevitable and began to lope beside him. As he ran, he tried to think of his options. The local spaceport was 40 klicks away. He wasn't in his fighting prime anymore, but he could make it in five hours at a steady jog. He wasn't sure Duke could, though, and he wasn't going to abandon her. If they had to stop and rest her, so be it.

So engrossed in his calculations was he that he almost made a second lieutenant mistake—he lost track of the bigger picture. He rounded the bend in the middle path as it approached Row 8 where the bulk of the pyro berries were grown, and came to a dead stop. Ahead of him, was the Gustavsons' farm, or more accurately, what was left of it. Their single-crop fields of corn were flattened, almost every stalk gone. Attacking the last few meters had to be thousands of the enemy plants. Within a few minutes, they would be crossing over into his property. Either these plants were larger cousins of the ones he'd seen on his property earlier or they had grown. These had to be a meter tall.

Duke whined beside him as he lifted his gaze. He didn't know the reclusive Gustavsons well, but their house was visible from his farm. It took him a moment to find it, or what was left of it. Half of a single wall still stood. The rest was a jumble of rubble.

How the hell. . . ?

The enemy plants, which were uprooting the Gustavsons' corn, weren't that big. If this was all there was to them, if they didn't have some sort of tools, how could they have destroyed a house? It didn't seem possible.

Ever the practical soldier, Colby had to accept what his eyes told him, even if his mind protested the impossibility. Their house was gone. And if the enemy could destroy their house, it could destroy his.

Colby started running back, this time with Duke pulling forward on her leash. At the corner of Row 6, he took a left and ran to the high point of the western half of the property. It didn't give him a panoramic view, but in every direction he could see a mass of enemy plants advancing on him.

"Looks like we're surrounded, girl," he said in a matter-of-fact voice.

This wasn't the first time this had happened to him. On Proclyn 301, his battalion had been surrounded by a division of the Gannon Imperial Army. It had taken the Marines 42 days and 73 percent casualties to break the siege, but break it they had.

"And you're no Imperial Cybotroopers," he shouted out before turning to Duke and saying, "Let's go see what we can do about this."

He ran back up to the compound. The enemy had already reached Row 3, some 400 or so meters away. He could hear them tearing into his crops.

Bolting into the vault, he stopped and ordered his thoughts. He had to figure out a way to stage a breakout, to get beyond the line of advancing plants. As a commissioned officer, Colby had been infantry, but he'd also been prior-enlisted with a combat engineer Military Occupational Specialty. As a combat engineer, he knew how to blow things up.

With his engineer kit, he had dozens of ways to pulp the enemy. Unfortunately, kits like that were not available to civilians, not even retired generals.

No problem, Edson, you'll just have to gyver it. OK, first what to make?

Combat engineers used a variety of explosives on their missions. Low explosives were used to move thing like dirt, high explosives to shatter and destroy objects. Colby would like nothing better than to use HE to destroy all the enemy in an area, giving Duke and him a clear path, but as he looked around the vault, he didn't have the time nor ready materials to create an HE bomb. What he did have, however, was fertilizer.

An ANFO it is, then.

The primary ingredient in an ANFO is ammonium nitrate, and that was also a main ingredient in fertilizer. He stepped up to the corn mixture and read the text under the red skull and crossbones on the side.

There! Ammonium nitrate, his pulse raced with excitement until he read the rest of the ingredients. *Fuck! Urea!*

Ammonium nitrate will not explode if it is mixed with common ingredients such as urea or ammonium sulfate, two typical additives to AN-based fertilizers for just that reason. He quickly checked the next cylinder, the one for pyro-berries. It wasn't any good, either. Each mixture had the needed AN, but not in a high enough concentration or without the additives that made it useless as an explosive.

He stepped back, hands on his hips, trying to figure out a solution. Then, he remembered his two specialty fields, the ones in which he grew the winter melons, raspberries, and other rare foods for his own consumption and to trade for meats. He didn't have one single cylinder for each of those—his fertilizer was mixed in the magnetic agitator and applied by a man-packed sprayer. He opened the pantry and pulled out a pack of Señor Fukimaru's Wonder Grow. The ingredient list started off with aluminum nitrate salts—and without any of the other ingredients that would render them inert. With a thrill, Colby grabbed another 5kg pack and put them on his workbench.

Now, he needed fuel and a detonator. Normally, the fuel would be a carbon-based liquid, such as gasoline or diesel. His farm, though, ran on electricity. He didn't have liquid fuel.

But I do have photovoltiac cells, though. And what do I paint on the back of the new ones? Aluminum powder paste! Aluminum powder and aluminum nitrate makes ammonal. Boom!

The cells that produced electricity were pretty foolproof, but they could be damaged by weather. Because he was a long way from a tech he had a small stock of the cells on hand for repairs. They'd been ready to go before he took over the property, so he hoped he still had the paste that had been used to paint the backs. He returned to the house and rummaged around the pantry shelves, trying to find some. He'd just about given up when he found a stained can which had obviously been opened previously. He carefully pried up the lid, and to his relief, there was at least half a can of the powder remaining.

Better still, he could use the can as a body for his bomb. What he didn't know was the proper percentage of AN to aluminum powder. He automatically tried pulling up the information on the net, but it was still down. His implant, however, contained some 10 terabytes of information, everything for the Marine seeking to perform almost any mission. Within moments, not only did he have the numbers, but a nice recording on how to mix the two. Minutes later, he had what he hoped was a working ammonal bomb.

Except for a detonator. This won't go off without one.

That might be a little more difficult, he realized. His farm had long been terrascaped to maximize productivity, so there wasn't a need for construction equipment. But the fuel and explosive needed something to set them off. He searched the vault, racking his brain for a solution, all the time noting that time was running out. He considered running out to the silos; grain silos have been known to explode and had dampening systems installed to prevent that. but he had no idea as to what mechanism in them set them off.

There's got to be something here I can use, but what?

He queried his implant, scanning through a list of military detonators until he came to field expedient measures. There were at least twenty, but all took time to prepare, time he didn't have. Finally, one caught his eye. If the tolerances were not too tight, it might work. He grabbed a small glass bottle of sulfuric acid, his half-made bomb, and bolted out the door. . .

. . . and came to a stop. To the east, the enemy plants had almost reached his house.

"Come on, Duke! No time to waste."

Duke whined, then ran back into the vault while Colby bolted back to the house and to the kitchen.

Please, please, be enough, he begged as he reached for the matches he kept above the stove.

The power in the house was electric, but he'd grown fond of grilling meat outside, and for that, he needed old fashioned matches—and friction matches used potassium chlorate to ignite. He had about 30 left in the box.

I hope it's enough.

Snapping off the heads, he placed them in a small plastic bag before dumping a cup of sugar in as well, shaking it up. It was crude, and it probably wouldn't work, but he was running out of options.

Turning to his liquor cabinet, he carefully removed a highly polished wooden box, flipping open the lid. Nestled in a form-fitting silk-covered pad was a small 250ml flask of 2402 Martell Cognac. The bottle had cost him three weeks salary, and he'd been saving it for a special occasion. Without hesitation, he opened the flask and dumped the golden liquid down his sink. It was the flask he wanted. Handblown by retro-craftsmen in Iberia back on Earth, it was delicate, almost insubstantial, crystal. He carefully filled the flask one quarter of the way with the sulfuric acid, then started to place it in his bomb, intending to surround it with the sugar-potassium chlorate mixture. Despite how fragile the flask was, however, it was possible that the aluminum nitrate and aluminum powder mixture would cushion it after he threw it. He needed to make sure the flask broke, causing the sugar mixture to explode, thereby setting off the rest of the bomb.

He opened the cabinet with his kitchenware and spotted his small salad bowl. It looked about right, and it just fit inside the aluminum powder can. Colby put in the sugar and match heads next, then lay the flask with the acid on top. The bowl was hard, the sides of the can were hard. He was sure that when it hit the ground, the flask would break. Whether the match heads would ignite and explode was another story, but this was the best he could do. He carefully closed the can, sealing the ingredients inside.

Colby ran back outside. The plants were in the compound, a dozen or so up against the east wall of his house, their leafy branches hugging the walls like nature-lovers communing with trees. He ran to the north side of the compound, ready to blast a hole in the incoming horde, but stopped. Duke had left him to run back to the vault, but he couldn't leave her. With a sigh, he ran back. The dog was cowering behind the cylinders, and he had to drag her out using the still attached leach.

She put up a fight, but he simply overpowered her.

There was a cracking sound as he dragged Duke back to the north side of the compound. A chunk of his house broke off under the assault of the plants. They might be much slower than him, but like a tree buckling pavement with their roots, they evidently had immense power.

More had entered the compound, but for the moment, they seemed to be ignoring Duke and him. He wasn't going to test them, however, and stayed as far away as he could as he got into position, ready to blast a path to freedom.

As he took in the sheer numbers of the enemy, though, he began having second thoughts. His little homemade bomb didn't seem like enough. But it was all he had.

Duke was jerking wildly at her leash, whining and barking. Colby jerked back, almost knocking her off her feet. He didn't need a panicking dog while he had a homemade bomb in his hands.

"He who will not risk, cannot win," he said, quoting an ancient wet-water navy hero, one of the many quotes that adorned the walls of the Officer Training School auditorium back on New Mars.

There was one more thing he could do. His Marine Corps utilities were sturdy, able to take a lot of punishment in addition to normal wear and tear. When the bullets were flying, however, they needed the body armor that was intertwined with the uniform's cloth. With a quick command, a tiny current activated that caused the armor fibers to align, making them impenetrable to small arms fire. He felt a little foolish activating the armor when faced with plants, but he was of the better-safe-than-sorry school of thinking.

He shifted the leash to his left hand, transferring the handle of the bomb to his right. He swung it around, building momentum until he released it to arc up in the air. Like an idiot, he stood there, feeling elation as it flew straight for the densest concentration of the plants he could see. He really didn't think it would work, and so was surprised that as it hit, there was a huge explosion, strong enough to blow him back on his ass.

"Ooh-rah!" he shouted, scrambling back up to his feet, ears ringing, but none the worse for the shock wave.

Below him, pieces of green littered the area around a 15-meter-wide hole in what had been hop-beans. Chunks of the enemy had reached him, torn apart by the blast. His little bomb might not have the brisance of a military HE bomb, but it had packed a lot of power. As strong as the enemy seemed to be, they couldn't stand up to pure brute force.

"Let's go," he shouted at Duke, pulling at her and starting down into the blast zone.

He didn't get far, pulling up into a stop as beyond the zone, enemy plants were rising from where they'd been blown flat. Colby had once seen a time-lapse video of sunflowers back on Earth following the sun, turning to keep their faces oriented to it. This was what he was seeing right then. The plants didn't have a flower, but there was no doubt in his military mind that they were turning to face him. If they had been ignoring him before, he was certainly the center of their attention now. As they started converging on him, he knew he wasn't about to break through to the north—or to any direction.

"Shit, Duke, back to the vault!"

The dog didn't need any encouragement. She bolted, almost pulling him along with her. They passed the silos, but as they approached the vault, the plants surged forward to cut them off. Colby let go of the leash, and Duke darted ahead, just out of reach of the forward edge of the plants. A couple of steps behind her, he wasn't going to be so lucky.

He wasn't going down without a fight, however. As the first plant moved to block him, he leveled a kick that sent the plant flying ten meters.

He felt his warrior take over as he leveled a second kick, breaking leafy branches off another.

"I'm going to make it," he said as he broke through, and darted just ahead of the advancing line.

Ten meters away from the door, something tripped him, and he ate a facefull of dirt. He twisted around, and one of the plants had wrapped its arm-like branches around his left ankle. He tried to kick it off him, but the branches started squeezing. Colby immediately understood how the things had started to take apart his house. It was like being caught in a compression vice. Without his body armor, he was sure his leg would be crushed, and whatever the first tiny plant had done to his hand when he'd picked it up would be repeated. He pushed with his right leg and managed to scoot forward, dragging his attacker with him as the pain mounted. He pushed off again, then four or five of the plants grabbed his attacker. Their combined effort started to pull him back. Colby clawed the ground for purchase, but he was being overpowered.

A flash of gold shot past his face. With a growl worthy of a wolf, Duke sunk her teeth in the main stalk of the plant latched on his leg. To his immense, but welcomed surprise, the plant released him, recoiling to about half of its length.

Colby jumped to his feet, grabbed Duke's leash, and bolted for the vault door as the rest of the plants rallied to converge on him. He darted though the door, then slammed it shut, bolting it.

Duke looked up at him, tail wagging.

"I owe you, girl, big time," he said as he tried to catch his breath, adrenaline flowing through him.

He'd tried to create an egress route, but all it seemed to do was to piss the plants off, assuming they even had the capability for that emotion. The way they'd reacted, especially when several of them had tried to help the one on his leg, had convinced him they were not mindless automatons, much more than simple biological weapons. He'd bet on the fact that they were individuals of some sort, at least.

"At least they're not invincible," he said. "We sure blew the crap out of some of them. Now I've just got to figure out how to do that again, but on a larger scale."

There was a thump from outside the vault. Duke growled as the hair on the back of Colby's neck stood on end. He'd seen the plants starting to tear apart his house. There was a big difference between his home and the vault, however. The house was built from Mennyboard, which was essentially compressed cellulose. Cheap and easy to make, it was sturdy enough for most purposes and could stand up to routine weather, but the building was hardly a fortress. The vault, on the other hand, was built to withstand a possible explosion of any of the chemicals it contained, and it was a shelter from extreme weather conditions. It would take quite a bit more effort to tear it down. He turned his attention back to trying to make a bigger bomb—although not before finding a long-handled shovel to keep readily at hand.

He went through the entire vault, comparing the ingredients and materials at hand to what his implant fed him about making explosives. Given six or seven hours, if the vault held up, he should be able to create a more powerful explosive, but would it be big enough to wipe out the plants? He didn't think so. He could make a type of napalm, but he had no way to deliver it.

Too bad. I bet they'd burn like old Christmas trees.

The image of the thousands of meter-tall plants going up in flames was appealing, and while he searched for a response, his mind kept drifting back to that image. But there was no way to bring flames to them. The farm had the heaters, of course, to protect the crops from cold snaps, but while each heater put out about 600,000 BTU per hectare/hour, which was pretty hefty, it was hardly a conflagration. Unless he could convince the plants to march into each heater in turn, they wouldn't do much. He couldn't even let the methane that powered the heating units build up. The gas-activated sensors on the heater automatically fired the ignitors when the methane first reached them.

But what if I could deactivate the sensors somehow?

"Ralph, can I run methane through the lines but deactivate the heating units?"

"Negative. Doing so would cause a dangerous buildup of gas with possible catastrophic consequences."

That's what I'm trying to do, idiot.

"I want to override that. Deactivate the heating units."

"I'm sorry, but Civil Code 4008.4.10 expressly forbids that while the system is online. Tampering with the heating units carries a 100,000 credit fine."

"So, it's possible to do it?" he asked, his interest rising.

"Affirmative. Each heating unit has a manual cut-off switch. The valve can then be opened to flush the system."

His excitement dropped off. In order to do that, he'd have to go out among the fields, something he doubted the plants would let him do.

"So, there is no way to do it from here?"

"Technically, yes, there is. But Civil Code 4008—"

"Stop," he ordered, not wanting to hear the AI continue.

"Can you override the farm AI?" he subvocalized to his implant.

A normal civilian implant wouldn't be able to force an AI to break a law, but high-level military units had more capabilities.

"Yes, that is possible," it replied.

"Do it. I want the heating units deactivated."

A moment later, his implant said, "Three of sixty-four units deactivated."

Colby's heart fell.

"Only three?"

"The remaining units are no longer receiving signals. The probability is high that they no longer have unit integrity."

"You mean they're destroyed?"

"Yes."

Colby could ask his implant for more details, but it was programmed to give them only when queried. If it said the probability was "high," then that was good enough for him. And it was good news. If the units were destroyed, then they couldn't set off the gas before enough had built up to be effective. With only three units still intact, his plan, half-formed as it was, might have a chance at success.

The real question in his mind now was if the methane could actually be concentrated enough to take the farm up in flames. He checked the weather outside. With winds at 5 kph, that might be enough to blow the methane off the property before it could build up. He needed to somehow transform the gas into something "stickier," for lack of a better term.

He queried his implant, not expecting a solution, but one popped up, something far easier than he'd expected: magnesium stearate. The substance was essentially a soap, the same thing that caused soap scum in his tub. The farm used it to coat the inside of all the cylinders and tubing to ensure the ingredients, especially the powders, didn't stick to the containers. It was also a general lubricant for much of the farm's pieces of equipment.

If the stearate kept materials separated, it didn't make sense that he could mix it with a gas, but his implant instructed him to run it through the agitator, giving him the percentages of each substance. With more than a little trepidation, he put in the commands to run the methane and magnesium stearate through the agitator and out through the lines to flood the farm.

"Distribution lines are not intact," the AI informed him.

"Pull up a diagram."

He leaned forward to study the schematic. The bulk of the lines were still in place, but all were damaged to some extent or the other. Some indicated leaks while others had huge chunks of line torn out.

"The bastards have been busy," he muttered before asking his AI, "Ralph, how can I achieve the most coverage?"

A moment later, the schematic changed with the selected lines highlighted in blue. The AI had bypassed several lines that had been torn out close to the compound while leaving others in the distribution plan. The resultant coverage was complete, even if the concentration varied.

A large cracking sound filled the vault, and Colby grabbed the shovel, holding it aloft as Duke let out a throaty growl. There was another crack coming from the east wall, but nothing penetrated into the building.

Yet.

Still holding the shovel, he ordered the AI to start the distribution, half-expecting to hear another protest that doing so violated some civil code, but Ralph acknowledged the order. He looked back to make sure the flow of both methane and magnesium stearate had begun, and the readouts on the control suite confirmed that. A green feed light indicated the mixture was being pushed down the lines.

Colby had learned more than he'd wanted to about explosions over the last half-an-hour. He'd never heard of the term "stoichiometric proportion," which was the concentration of the flammable material in the air at a given temperature and pressure that gave the most bang-for-the-buck. What he did know was that he wasn't going to achieve that with his gyvered system. He needed to reach the LEL, or Lower Explosive limit. For methane, that was 5 percent. Despite the huge repository of data in his implant, he couldn't find what the LEL was for a methane-stearate mix. He didn't even understand what the 5 percent LEL meant; it was not something as simple as meaning 5 percent of the atmosphere. He tried to follow the math before giving up. He didn't need to know what it meant. If the sensors on the remaining three heating units worked, all he had to know was when the meters read 5 percent. Or in this case, 10 percent, the buffer he was giving himself to take into consideration the addition of the magnesium stearate.

There were more cracking sounds from the walls. The plants were making progress even on the vault. Colby just hoped the building could hold out.

"There we go, Duke. It's working," he said when Unit 14 indicated a jump in methane. It was only at .5 percent, but it was a start.

Duke whomped her tail on the floor.

More to keep busy than anything else, Colby gathered the materials to make a Molotov Cocktail, something he could have done in his sleep. He intended on using the three heating units to set off the explosion, but it was always a good idea to have a back-up.

Slowly, the methane concentration started to rise. Unit 14 hit 5 percent within ten minutes, with 23 at 3 percent. There was no feedback at all from Unit 33. With 14 and 23 covering a third of the farm at best, he wouldn't know how well the coverage was getting to be on the rest of the property.

He waited, one hand on Duke's back and chewing the fingernails of the other, trying to will the readouts of the two working sensors to rise faster, but after reaching 8 percent, Unit 14 seemed stuck. Unit 23 kept rising, but at a glacially slow pace.

There was a louder crack in the wall, and pieces of the inner wall broke free. Colby jumped to his feet while Duke stood beside him, her head held low while she fiercely growled. He slowly stalked forward, shovel held out, until he stood before the wall. Poking it, he knocked away the inner wall covering. He was now staring at the structural body of the wall, a solid-looking piece of some metallic alloy. As he watched, it warped, twisting before his eyes. He wasn't an engineer, but that had to be a tremendous amount of force to actually warp it. Suddenly, whatever feeling of security he had vanished. He knew that if he merely tried to wait the enemy out, he'd fail. They would break into his fortress. His plan had to work if he and Duke were going to get out alive.

He went back to the display. Unit 14 was still stuck on 8 percent, but 23 was at 7 percent. Unit 23 was at the third highest piece of property on the farm, a good 15 meters higher than the lowest point. Even "thickened" gas would tend to flow downhill, so common sense told him that the concentrations were probably higher at the other points.

But the Gustavsons' farm is lower than mine, he realized in a flash. *I bet I'm losing methane to them.*

He checked his methane supply. He was down to 23 percent. The methane was produced in-house in the digestion tank behind the vault. It was still being fermented, but it was draining at a far greater rate. He'd be out soon.

A rending screech filled the vault, and the entire building shook. Colby ran back to the east wall, tearing away the inner coverings. At the northeast corner, behind the racks of cylinders, four rivets had popped out. He couldn't see daylight, but it was only a matter of time now, a very short time.

Shit. I've got to give it a shot now.

He took a deep breath, then said, "Ralph, turn on the heater ignitors."

His AI might have had a problem with turning the ignitors off, but it didn't have one with turning them on.

"Confirm," it said as Colby held his breath, drawing Duke into his arms.

And nothing happened.

There was no explosion, no anything.

"Ralph, did you initiate the ignition."

"Affirmative. There was no confirmation return to indicate compliance."

"So, they didn't go off?"

"That is a possibility. Another possibility is that the confirmation circuits are down."

"What's the probability that it was the ignitors that malfunctioned rather than there being a problem with the circuits?"

"There isn't enough data to calculate an acceptable figure."

The noise coming in from the outside grew louder, but he pushed it out of his mind. He had to make a decision. There had been no explosion of fire. That could be because his plan was faulty, because it was a good plan but the concentration of methane was not great enough, or because the ignitor failed to set off the initial explosion. He had two options: wait until the concentration increased (or he ran out of methane) or try his Molotov Cocktail. He checked the display; he was at 19 percent of his methane supply. As the supply decreased, so would the flow out the lines. Too slow, and the methane hugging the ground out there would flow or be blown off the property faster than it was being replenished.

"Molotov it is, girl," he said.

He picked up the bomb, checking it over one more time. It seemed to be in order. The wick, which was a twisted rag, should burn long enough for the bomb to hit the ground and burst open. If there was enough methane out there, it would ignite. It was that simple.

With it in one hand, the shovel in the other, he walked up to the door, leaning the shovel up against the wall and placing that hand's palm against the door itself. He could feel vibrations. He didn't know whether that meant the plants were attacking the door or the vibrations were transmitted from the attacks on the east and north side of the building.

"Only one way to find out, girl," he said, placing the Molotov Cocktail on the ground at his feet and putting his shoulder to the door.

One. . . two. . . three, he counted to himself before hitting the latch and pushing with all his might.

And he hit resistance. He got the door opened halfway, shoving several of the plants to the side. He knew nothing of the enemy's physiology, but he could have sworn that the things registered surprise for a moment before they reacted.

Colby reacted quicker, though. He grabbed the shovel and stepped forward, swinging it like the Grim Reaper's scythe. He cut down two of the plant creatures, toppling them, and knocked back several more, clearing a small space for himself. He lunged back for the Molotov Cocktail, lit the wick, and with two hops forward, launched it towards the west, trying for the lowest section of the farm he could reach. As the bomb arched up in the air, the rotten egg smell of the odorant added to methane registered in his brain. He hadn't purposefully released any methane around the house, but enough had flowed in for him to smell it. If it had been above the LEL right there, he'd have just blown himself up.

If he could smell it, then a big enough explosion could ignite the compound. He jumped back and grabbed the door, hoping to slam it shut, but several of the plants had other ideas. Green branches reached forward to hold the edge of the door. One branch latched onto his arm while Duke started to dart forward, teeth bared.

And the world exploded. A huge fist hit the door, slamming it shut and sending Colby flying across the floor on his ass. He hit the base of the first cylinder rack and lay there, stunned. The door to the outside started to swing open a crack as heat and smoke poured into the vault. Still dazed, he managed to get to his feet and stumble to the door, pulling it shut and locking it. Bits and pieces of plant arms, cut off when the door shut, lay on the floor. One larger chunk was slowly moving. Without much thought, he picked up the shovel, put the blade against the meatier part of the plant, and stepped on it, cutting the piece in two. Green goo squirted out, but it lay still.

"You OK, girl?" he asked, his voice sounding as if he was underwater.

Duke gave out a plaintive whine, but thumped her tail on the floor.

Colby knew that his plan had worked, but to what extent? He had no eyes on the farm, and given the temperatures being recorded from the vault's roof sensors, the entire place was on fire. He and Duke weren't going anywhere for the time being.

Ever the pragmatist, and still somewhat dazed, he lay down for a nap, Duke's head across his stomach. He knew people who'd had concussions weren't supposed to sleep, but there wasn't anyone around to scold him for that. He awoke a few hours later, his mind feeling much clearer. Immediately, he tried the net again, but once more, he couldn't connect. For all he knew, the planet could be razed and he and Duke the only survivors.

He stood up and checked the temperature outside. While still a few degrees higher than normal, he knew he could survive. With Duke on his heels, he went back to the door, kicking the pieces of enemy plants to the side. He put an ear to the door, not knowing what to expect, but he heard nothing.

"Might as well get this over," he told Duke as he pushed open the door.

"Son-of-a-bitch," he said as he surveyed the charred landscape.

The entire compound was blackened and covered with what had to be plant corpses. He shifted his gaze over to what were the remains of his house. He couldn't tell if the plants had destroyed it or the fire, but it was definitely gone. With Duke following, he walked down the line of silos, the twisted remains telling him the plant creatures had destroyed them before the fires had done their work.

The enemy remains became less substantial as he wandered to the western side of the compound where utterly devastated fields stretched below him, the ashes of enemy plants and pyro berry bushes indistinguishable from each other. The destruction didn't end at his property line. Flames had made their way across the Gustavsons' fields to their house, which still smoked. Beyond that, black smoke of an active fire rose into the air.

Colby knew that his methane mixture couldn't have flowed that far, and if it had, the LEL would have been too small to ignite. But sometimes wildfires grew from the tiniest of sparks, and if each farm's firefighting system was knocked out, then they could grow unchecked.

Without a word, Colby turned and walked back to the rubble that had been his house. He paused for a moment at what had been the front door, then with a sigh, stepped over the jam. There was nothing left. Duke bounded past him and started nosing around what had been the kitchen. He started to call her back, but then stopped. If she found something to eat, all the more power to her, and she was smart enough to avoid anything hot enough to burn her.

He kicked a partially melted support beam out of the way and walked to the back of the house. This had been where his I Love Me wall had been, the culmination of his long career as a Marine. All of it was gone, now, and it felt as if that career had only been a dream. His eye caught a rectangular object on the ground, and he bent over to pick it up. It was a plaque from his first battalion as a second lieutenant. The top of the plaque had burned away, but enough of the bottom had survived that he could read "Second Lieutenant Colby Edson, Fair Winds and Following Seas from the Magnificent Bastards."

Half of a burned plaque wasn't much to show for 51 years of service. With a shrug, he dropped it to the ground with the rest of the junk.

Interlude I: Spores, Before and After

Like a dormant seed within its pod, the Gardener dreamed. It waited in its vessel high above the planet, lost in contemplation as it luxuriated in the steady stream of data carried up from the atmosphere below. No slightest glint or gleam of energies spilled from within the vessel. No signal slipped out from its shell. The Gardener itself had designed the meta-cellulose that enclosed its home in space so as to render the vessel undetectable by its own kind, leaving it free to work without interruption. With visionary intensity it had painstakingly shaped the code underlying every gene for both optimization and aesthetics. The vessel could sense, react, absorb, ignore, and otherwise respond to both minimal and extreme gravimetric forces, as well as a broad range of hostile radiation. Out of a sense of ambition, it had nurtured the specifications to endure encounters in proximity to a gas giant, though of course it would never venture to such a world. What need for a

Gardener where no garden could grow? But this world, a planet it had only visited twice before, most recently some two hundred of its revolutions ago, this world offered its vessel neither threats nor challenges.

Or so the Gardener had presumed.

Passive mappings had flowed into the vessel as the planet completed several rotations below, revealing crude, right-angled distributions of vegetation, the sort of blocky plantings that a newly sprouted child might make, in stark contrast to the graceful fractal distributions the Gardener had seeded during its last visit. But children were not permitted to stray into the gardens of adults, let alone possess the experience to create a vessel to take them so far from home.

Other problematic signs had demanded its attention as well. Patterns of erosion, oceanic oxygen levels, and historic indications of rain density—each individually improbable but nonetheless plausible particulars—combined to hint that one or more other beings had come and placed their imprint upon this world. Imbeciles, judging by the data. Or worse, a Gardener who had put forth its own sense of the artistic instead of creating in tune to the universe's whispers. Such things occurred, albeit rarely. It had caught word of just this sort of radical movement when it last tasted the soil of home. There were few enough Gardeners, and fewer still who chose to share their work in space, that even a pod's worth could produce unsavory excuses for gardens amidst the otherwise barren planets and moons of the galaxy. And yet, surely, even such radicals would not presume to intervene on a claimed world.

No, another factor was in play here. Over the span of several more rotations, the Gardener had turned its attention to gathering preliminary chromatography data. It had even repeated the initial analysis, but the outcome remained unchanged. The perfect garden it had seeded during its last visit now exhibited the presence of complex toxins that could not exist in nature. They ruled out the possibility of even the most extreme and iconoclastic of Gardeners or even any of the weak imitators scattered among the lesser races of the galaxy. Only a single explanation existed: Meat.

Every Gardener knew that a certain amount of meat was necessary to maintain proper atmospheric balance. Anaerobic gardens were certainly possible, some portions were actually elegant, but real complexity and biodiversity required a synergy of gases, and one could only go so far with plankton. It was the classic tradeoff, allowing larger and more complex invertebrates—and even vertebrates—into a garden could lead to a lush outcome, but time and again animal life proved itself a nuisance. The Gardener had observed similar patterns among its peers' creations, some pesky vertebrate evolving over the course of millennia until it achieved a pathetic proto-sapience, and with it, invariably, a compulsion to either alter the perfection of the environment or simply overbreed until it poisoned its habitat with its own wastes.

But this was different. Millennia had not passed, barely two hundred revolutions. Animal evolution did not advance at such rates, even in as idyllic an environment as it had put in motion before leaving. Moreover, the other signs of proto-sapient pests— alteration and degradation of the landscape in pursuit of mineral resources, erection of crude and short-lived structures, pollution of rivers as a consequence of early industry—none of these had occurred in significant density or frequency, or so the vessel's passive scans suggested.

Data would continue to pour in the longer it remained in orbit, but even at this stage it had detected only a single, major, artificial structure where none should exist. Enhanced optics might well reveal smaller constructions in the vicinity of the crude patches that marred its carefully designed plantings, and indeed, patterns and concentrations among the air vectors had implied these locations were the source for the toxins that had been introduced to its world.

Was it possible? Had the Meat despoiling its garden arrived from outside? Could Meat ever achieve sufficient sophistication as to travel between worlds? Fantastic as the idea might be, the stuff of nightmares and madness, how else to account for the data?

Deep within the husk of its navigational locker, the Gardener had stirred. Left to its own tendencies, vegetable nature preferred patience and slow change. Its own species evolution into motility had been weighed and discussed for ages before embracing the opportunities of choice and direction it afforded. Yes, they could now venture off world, travel into space and apply their vision to craft new gardens, but even so, all Gardeners sought stillness. In this next phase of gardening this planet, it had expected to spend fifty or more revolutions tweaking and pruning, and never having to physically move. Already the Meat had pushed it out from its comfort zone.

In response to a pulsed signal, its husk had split and the Gardener had emerged. Green tendrils shot forth from its core forming ropey limbs, reinventing the motility it had shed upon entering the navigation locker. Even as carefully grown a thing as its vessel could not be allowed to handle all operations remotely; some few tasks required direction attention. It had slid and sloped its way to a subsection of the vessel, triggering long dormant processes.

The Meat would have to be eradicated. Whatever flawed plantings it had devised would be razed to make way for the resumption of the original design. The crude shelters that Meat always seemed so fond of would be pulled apart, sundered down to constituent pieces, and these pieces further reduced to their basic elements with the help of a few revolutions of erosion until they were reclaimed by the soil. And the offending toxins would be absorbed by carefully designed vegetable tools programmed to encapsulate every molecule, removing it from interaction with the rest of the environment until the Gardener could deploy other tools to spirit the foulness away. If the Meat happened to be razed or sundered or otherwise destroyed in the process, that, too, would be just a part of weeding one's garden.

The Gardener had consulted its records of past work, made adjustments, and instructed its vessel to manufacture and disperse several loads of spores strategically so the prevailing air patterns would carry them to the Meat's locations of disruption during the planet's dark cycle. The basic resources needed by all organic life existed in abundance on this world, even in those places where Meat had gained hold. With the warmth of morning the spores had sprouted into purge agents, quickly achieved sufficient mass to acquire a rudimentary motility, and begun carrying out the directives the Gardener had encoded in them.

By the end of the next day cycle, its garden was back on track, leaving only a single, major structure with which to deal. An additional rotation's worth of data indicated electromagnetic concentrations that did not belong in its garden, suggesting the possibility of an incursion of Mechanical pseudo-life. Irritating as that might prove, such an outcome made more sense than postulating the mysterious arrival of proto-sapient Meat. Moreover, the protocols for disabling mechanicals were well established. The Gardener keyed the creation and programming of a few billion additional spores, similar to purge agents but with combinatorial capabilities. Their insertion into the atmosphere would land them in a tight ring around the offending structure. As they quickened and took form, they'd encircle the target, establishing containment, and then advance, rending any inorganics in their path. Meat or Mechanical, all would be purged, the offending structure dismantled, and the insufferable electromagnetics eliminated.

Afterwards, the Gardener would need to allocate time to study the data in order to learn the origin of such an affront, but best to resolve it first. And too, time was always on vegetation's side, a concept Mechanicals could not appreciate and which Meat would never be able to grasp. Pleased with its efforts, the Gardener perambulated back to its navigation locker and drew the walls tight around itself, bonding once more with the living green of its vessel. Leaving the spores to do their work, it returned to the pleasures of contemplation.

Part II: Reinforcements and Retreat

"Come on, Erin, I really need to talk to the Dickhead," Colby said.

"You shouldn't call the vice minister that, General. You know that. But I told you, he isn't taking your call."

"Did you ask him face-to-face? And what did he say?"

There was a pause, then, "I don't want to repeat it."

"Tell me, Erin."

"It wasn't nice, General."

"I'm a big boy. Tell me."

"Well, OK. He said he that you are a worthless piece of shit who should rot in hell."

It took a moment for that to sink in. He knew that Vice Minister Asahi Salinas Greenstein hated him, but this went beyond the pale. This was a matter of security, not petty politics. Besides, the vice minister had won. He wasn't the one exiled to a backwater agricultural planet at the edge of human space.

When Colby had uncovered the corruption at the highest levels, the siphoning of war supplies to personal accounts, he'd thought the vice minister would have led the pack to throw the criminals into prison. He hadn't realized the depth of the corruption or how high it went. When he'd been given the choice between resigning or being court-martialed over trumped up charges, he'd wanted to fight. It wasn't until the threat of levying charges against his loyal subordinates that he'd given in and taken the poison pill.

He took a deep breath to calm himself. He couldn't afford to get the vice minister's personal secretary upset with him as well.

"Erin, I'm going to record what I've observed here, all of it. If I've still got the connection, I'll upload it to you. Please, please, get that to the Di. . . to the vice minister, or if not him, to General Tybor. This is important."

"I'll forward it up, General. But with the resumption of hostilities with the Borealis Pact, some agricultural pest isn't going to be high on anyone's priorities."

Colby wanted to scream his frustration, but he damped that down.

"Just do what you can, Erin, OK? I've got to go now."

He cut the connection, fuming. He was trying to report an invasion, because after examining what little was left of the marauding plants, he was convinced that they were not some lab experiment gone wrong but a full-scale alien attack.

He'd been lucky just to make it through to his old boss. Communications, both on Vasquez and off-planet, had been cut. With the full capabilities of his implant, that wouldn't have been a problem, but his implant had been stripped of those when he'd left the service. It had only been through some convoluted routing and hacking that his implant had been able to route the call through the local wormhole's comms bot and back to New Mars, and then only to Erin's public line. His implant estimated that he had fewer than 400 seconds before the bot's AI caught up to his implant's machinations, realized there had been a hack, and closed off the pipeline. Colby's call had taken 405 seconds before he cut it off. Now, his best course of action was to record everything he'd seen, send it up as a pulse upload, then trust Erin to get it to the right person.

He'd stood up to go back into the vault, and Duke jumped to her feet, tail wagging as she looked up at him.

"Sorry, girl. I'll try to find you something to eat, but I want to check the progress on the precipitate."

Colby hadn't simply sat around all night in the vault. He'd known he'd been lucky with both his ANFO bombs and the methane. They'd been made on the fly, and the fact that they'd worked was nothing short of a miracle. He might have beaten back the assault, but that was only a battle, and the war might still be ongoing. If that was the case, he needed to be better prepared, so with his implant's guidance, he'd been busy preparing better and stronger weapons. He'd already produced a better flammable jelly-substance that now filled two cylinders, complete with jury-rigged dispensers. They were bulky and heavy, but he thought they'd make passable flamethrowers. One task that took time, however, was to precipitate pure potassium chlorate from bleach. He'd been too lucky with the match heads setting off the detonator, so he needed to improve that.

The process required to produce the potassium chlorate he needed released chlorine, so he wanted to precipitate the crystals outside, but he didn't have a power source out there, and he'd had to do it inside the vault, but under the hood. This was actually the second step in the process, what his implant termed "fractional crystallization," and he was more than pleased to see that the reaction looked to be completed. With the pure crystals, he could finish detonators for the almost-completed bombs he had prepared. An hour later, he had 30 powerful grenades lined up, ready to use. He carefully packed them into empty storage cases, then stacked them up by the door.

He felt a sense of accomplishment, something he hadn't experienced since he'd arrived on the planet.

Let the bastards come again! I'm ready!

Duke had been sitting alongside the wall, watching his every move. He felt guilty. The old girl had come to his defense, and he'd been ignoring her. His house was destroyed, but he should be able to scrounge up some food for her.

"Come on, girl, let's go see what we can find."

With her on his heels, he left the vault. As he crossed the compound, he opened the planetary comms net, more from routine over the last 15 hours than from any hope of hearing from anyone, so he was surprised when a voice said, "Mayday, Mayday, is anyone receiving this?"

"I am," he said automatically, then instantly regretted it.

In time of war, communications had to be limited. Even with scrambling messages, the mere fact that there was a transmission might give the enemy AIs information that they could use.

"Who is this?" the female voice asked.

Colby hesitated, but as he realized that this was obviously a human and not an invading plant, he said, "Colby Edson. I've got a farm in Guernsey. Thirty-one F."

"Oh, thank god! Are you OK? Were you attacked?"

"Affirmative," he answered, snapping into military-speak. "Who are you?"

"I'm Topeka Watanabe, assistant launch coordinator, and I need help."

Colby knew the name, of course. All of his crops, all of the crops in the continent, were slung into space from Blair de Staffney Station, and he'd seen her tagline on most of his receipts.

"What kind of help?"

"We've been attacked by the plant things. They killed Sestus, and Riordan's been hurt."

Riordan was the station director, but Colby had never heard of Sestus.

"We've been hit pretty hard out here in Guernsey, too. I don't think my neighbors made it, either. It looks like the attacks have stopped, though."

It was true. Colby had gone on a quick recon of the area that morning after emerging from spending the night in the vault. There wasn't any sign of the plants, at least not living ones. This wasn't only in the burned area of his farm; it was everywhere. All of the vegetation within sight had been destroyed, as had all buildings and windmills, leaving only his vault intact—damaged, but intact. Outside of the scorched area he'd burned, there were rapidly decomposing bodies of the invaders, but nothing living.

"They've stopped for now, but there's a ship above us in orbit, and it isn't one of ours."

For a split second, Colby felt relief. A ship could take them off the planet. A ship would have comms back to New Mars or even Earth. But he also knew that no ship was scheduled for another two months, and Ms. Watanabe wouldn't be telling him she needed help if it was a human ship. Still, he had to ask.

"Is it alien?"

"You'd better fucking believe it. It matches nothing on the scans."

"So, you've got power?" he asked.

"I'm on back-up. Most of the station was destroyed. I've got the processing station and the cannon, and a few of the buildings are left. They did a number on us."

"I was a Marine Corps general—"

"I know who you are. And I need you here. It's your duty."

"Well, just hold on a minute. You're 30 klicks away, and I don't know if the way between us is clear of the enemy."

"It's clear."

"How can you be sure, Ms. Watanbe?"

"Because I saw them stop in the middle of their attack, then go off to die. Why don't you know that, I mean if you're alive, you must have seen it, too. They're dead there, right?"

"I've been in my vault since yesterday afternoon."

"And they let you alone? That's weird. I saw the monitors of what they did to the outlying farms around here. It wasn't pretty. The Pavonis, when the bastards came in their house, and Hermes tried to fight them, that was. . ." she said, trailing off.

"I beat them back," he interrupted, sensing she was getting into visuals that were better forgotten for the moment. "I burned them."

"No shit? You burned them? With what?"

"I made a kind of napalm," he said, not without a bit of pride.

"Then I really need you here, like now."

"But you said they're all dead. Why the urgency?"

"Because, that ship up there? It launched landers, thousands of them, and all are heading right here to the station!"

****

Two hours later, Colby brought the cargo pod to a halt as the station came into view. He'd loaded the pod with with his two flame throwers, his grenades, some extra chemicals, and, of course,

Duke. The pods were designed to transport crops to the station and bring back supplies, not for personal transport. It was awkward and snug, but it beat walking, which he'd assumed he'd have to do before he'd been able to repair one of the dead-lined pods. It had just enough power in the batteries to follow the inert telltales buried in the hover track to the station.

Even at this distance, he could see through the front-mounted cam that the enemy plants were already at the station, what had been a collection of four warehouses, a processing station, and the launch facility. Three of the warehouses had been broken down into rubble, and the plants looked to be swarming the processing station and the launch cannon. He couldn't be sure over the distance, and the damaged structures were of little use for comparison, but the enemy seemed bigger today.

"I'm at D2, Topeka," he passed over the comms, using her first name as she insisted. "How're you holding out?"

"About fucking time, General," she answered. "They've still got hard-ons for the cannon and factory."

The cannon was essentially a rail gun that launched the cargo pods into space and on an intercept course for the wormhole that took them to the huge distribution network on New Mars.

Although it wasn't designed for personnel, it could be used as a last-ditch emergency evacuation system in specially designed cargo pods. If the plants managed to take the cannon out of action, then neither of the two surviving humans (three, if you counted Riordan locked away in his medical chamber) was going to get off the planet until and if someone came charging to the rescue.

"I think they're keying in on the cannon and irradiation units in the factory," she added.

"Why do you think that?"

"It makes sense. What's the cannon but a big electromagnetic field? And the irradiation units, what powers them? It makes friggin' sense. I think they can detect them, 'cause that's right where they headed. I about crapped myself when they landed, seeing as you were taking your sweet time to get here, but they walked right on past me."

Colby ignored the not-so-subtle jab. Topeka might be outspoken and crude, but she'd been through a lot, and what she'd said about the plants made sense.

"Have you seen any movement to the south of your position?"

"My position? You mean in the house?"

"Where you're at now. At the launch facility."

The three station personnel's living quarters were above the facility's office and control center, so it made sense that they simply called it their "house," but he couldn't assume anything, not with these stakes.

"I'm not sure. I can't really just go for a stroll to see, you know. But I think it's probably clear."

He took a moment to observe the station compound. On the north side of the building, the cannon's rail lay on an east-west axis to take advantage of the clockwise rotation of the planet. He couldn't see too much detail from well over a klick away, but while the plant soldiers were all over the rail, the south side of the building looked clear.

"OK, this is what I'm going to do. I've got some weapons with me, and I'm not going to abandon them. I'm going to take my pod to Charlie's loading docks," he said, referring to the lone warehouse still standing."

"Can't," Topeka interrupted him. "The road's been too torn up. Your pod won't make it through. Just come here to the house, and I'll let you in."

That was getting too close to the enemy for comfort, but he had a bigger concern.

"No hover pads to take me there."

"Don't need them none. Get to D1, then uncouple your pod. You can trolley it from there to here."

"Uncouple it?" he asked, more than a little confused.

Once locked into the track, the pods followed the designated path, internal controls keeping them on course.

"Geez! You've been here how long, and you don't even know your equipment? Uncouple it. Just hit externals, then your pin, then 'Break Lock.'"

Colby hadn't known he could do that. In all fairness, he'd never had to. Once his pods left the farm, they were out of sight and out of mind. But if he could unlock the pod, then he should be able to guide it as it hovered over the ground.

"OK, I'm on my way," he said.

"Make it quick, General."

He didn't respond but started the pod up again. He was in plain sight of the enemy fighters, if they even had sight as he knew it, but he couldn't detect any sign that they were paying attention to him. At the farm, they hadn't focused on him until he'd tossed the ANFO bomb. Before that, it was as if he didn't exist, or as if he wasn't considered as important as pulling up his crops. That made no sense to him, but part of his training had been to try and understand his enemies. He could not accept that ignoring him was some random act. For the plants, there had to be a reason he'd been ignored until he'd revealed himself as someone who could cause them harm.

I hope the ones at the farm haven't been in contact with these guys, passing around my mugshot.

He reached D1 and stopped the pod. Following Topeka's instructions, he uncoupled it from the track.

"Here goes," he said to Duke, then popped the cover and stepped out.

He half expected some of the plants would turn towards him, but once again, it was as if he wasn't there. Just as well; these plants were indeed bigger, nearly his own height. He shrugged, thankful for their disinterest, and gave the pod a tug. The thing had to mass 3,000 kg, but it followed him like a puppy as he slowly made his way off the track and down to the footpath that led into the station. He passed a destroyed junction box of some kind, the twisted wreck and smashed foundation a testament to the raw strength of the plants.

Duke whined from inside the pod, but he ignored her. He didn't want her running around and drawing attention to him. He was too exposed as it was, and he kept his eyes scanning, ready to bolt and run at the first sign he was on the things' radar. They may be immensely strong, but he was quicker, and he was ready to put that quickness to use if needed.

But it wasn't needed. He made his way to the facility unopposed. The most difficult thing was to control the pod. It moved easily enough, but it packed a lot of momentum, and off the hover track, he crashed the thing into the remains of Warehouse B and the facility before he reached the door and called Topeka.

"About friggin' time, General," she said as she opened the door.

Colby didn't know what he expected based on her somewhat rough and in-your-face language, but whatever that was, she wasn't it. Petite with long black hair, she was young, possibly not even 50 years old. She looked like a school teacher, maybe, or a programmer. But there was a fire to her that almost danced out of her eyes. This woman meant business.

"So, what do you got in there that was so damned important?" she asked.

"Let's get it inside, and I'll show you," he said, ever conscious of the teeming plants bent on destruction just on the other side of the building.

She stepped back, sizing up the pod, then said, "I don't think so. It ain't gonna fit. No reason for a cargo pod to come in here, you know. We gotta unload it here."

He realized she was right, so he opened the top. Duke immediately jumped out, tail wagging.

"Shit, a dog? What the hell do you have a dog for?"

Colby immediately bristled and said, "She saved my ass back on the farm. I wasn't going to leave her."

Topeka shrugged, then said, "Fine, but what else do you got? What's with the feed cylinders?"

"I made them into flame throwers. The plants don't like fire," he said, feeling proud of his ingenuity.

She shrugged again, then said, "I hope they work. Let's get them unloaded." She grabbed one and tried to lift it, then said, "Holy shit! What's in them?"

"You take the boxes, but be careful. They're bombs. Grenades, more like, and I don't know how stable they are."

"Hell, I didn't call him here to blow me up," she muttered as she lifted the first box and took it inside.

Colby rolled the first flamethrower to the edge of the pod, then with a grunt, lifted it and lowered it to the deck. It was heavy, no lie, and he looked to see if Topeka had seen him lift it. He wasn't used to anyone giving him orders, and the young woman had a take-charge personality. A show of physical strength was in order, he thought, to reassert his position as a Marine general and in charge. She didn't seem to notice as she brushed past him to pick up another box.

He about popped a gut lifting the second flamethrower, but they had the pod unloaded within a couple of minutes. Topeka gave it a hard shove with her leg, and it drifted out of the way.

"OK," he said, trying to take charge. "If we let them destroy the cannon, we're stuck here. So, we have to take the fight to them. Either that, or we retreat and wait for rescue."

He didn't like the second option, but he felt obligated to mention it. She wasn't a Marine, and he didn't feel like he could order her into what would probably be a futile fight.

"If we retreat, Riordan's a dead man," she said bitterly. "We can't move him in the chamber, and if we take him out, he's a goner. Those fucking plant-things will tear this place down, chamber too. I can't leave him."

Colby felt a rush of respect. She understood the situation, and loyalty was more important than her own safety. He understood the sentiment—he just hadn't expected to see it in a government civilian.

"Those flamethrowers," she said, tilting her chin to point at them. "They gonna work?"

"They should, at least as long as the pressure stays high enough. The jelly, it'll stick to anything and burn like Hades' fire, but I had to use compressed air to load them. Once that runs out, well, we don't want the fire to back up into the cylinders now, do we."

She nodded, then said, "That'd not be a good idea."

"But until then, I think they'll work fine."

"Kinda heavy, though. In case you haven't noticed, I'm a bit on the small side. But, I think I got an idea. Can you wait here?"

"Where're you going?"

"Just wait. Five minutes, tops," she said before she opened the door, peeked in both directions, then slipped out.

What the hell? Where's she going?

He shook it off and started opening the cases with the ANFO grenades. He was very confident as to the 2.0 versions he'd made. Not only were they closer to foolproof, they should have a much bigger bang.

When that was finished, he looked around the room. Through a clear window in the back, he could see lights. Walking over, he saw the lights were from displays. This was the control room. There had to be at least internal power still running as five of the displays were active. A red light was flashing on the second display. Colby entered the room for a closer look, and his heart sank when he realized what was on the screen.

The plant soldiers, much larger than the ones that had attacked his farm, had managed to damage the immensely strong ceramalloy rails of the cannon. The display indicated that the entire cannon was on the verge of failure.

The outer door opened, and Colby spun around, ready for battle, but it was Topeka sticking in her head.

"Come take a look and tell me what you think," she said. "Can we use these for your flame-thrower contraptions?"

With a last glance at the display screen, he went to the door and looked out. Topeka had rustled up a forklift, one of several that must have been used at the station. Carried in the forks was a personal lift-assist.

"We had this in the repair shop right here," she said, pointing to a roll-up door further down the side of the building.

"That might work," Colby said, moving to sit in the lift.

"Have you used one of these?" she asked, blocking his way.

"Well, no. But how hard—"

"Doesn't matter if you can learn to use it. I can, so this is mine. You get the Daihatsu," she said, pointing to the personal lifting yoke.

He started to argue, but she was right.

"The cannon's about to fail," he said, changing the subject. "Anything we can do about it?"

"Shit, I thought it'd hold out longer," she said, as she dashed back into the control center, Colby on her tail.

"Well, I guess it's time," she said, more to herself, Colby thought, than to him.

"Time for what?"

"Time to make me some green mash," she said as she flowed into the control chair. Her hands flew over the switches as she vocalized some orders that made no sense to him. Several other displays came to life, and on one of the screens, a door opened.

"Is that a space pod?" Colby asked, despite recognizing it for what it was.

"Yep. It's been in the breach and ready for launch since the bastards attacked. We had eight more on deck, but they got themselves destroyed by our friends out there. So, this is it."

Colby immediately realized what she was going to do.

"What about the rail?" he asked, pointing to the monitor with the red flashing light.

She shrugged and said, "It'll work or not. But for sure, we're going to crush some of the fuckers."

"And if the damage to the rails is bad enough?"

"Then this baby's gonna be smashed all over the landscape," she said.

Which doesn't matter now, does it?

"Have at it," he said.

He watched the countdown, alarms deafening the control room while Topeka overrode each attempted shutdown.

"Here she goes!" she said as the charge released, sending the pod accelerating down the rail.

The plant soldiers had been working on the center of the rail, right in front of the control facility. By the short time the pod had reached the plants, it was already at nine kilometers per second. With over 3000 kgs of mass, that was an unstoppable force, and the air above the rail exploded into a green mist.

"Ooh-rah!" Colby shouted, unable to contain himself as he pounded on Topeka's back.

He didn't even notice that the space pod continued past the damaged area and made it to the ramp at escape velocity. Vasquez's last pod to go out would deliver its cargo as it was designed to do.

"I think that's green ick," Topeka said, reaching to the screen and touching an out-of-focus green spot that was on the cam lens.

"And I think you're right. You exploded the suckers!"

"Oh, and now I think we might have their attention."

Colby looked at the displays. The singular focus of the plant soldiers had been broken. A good number seemed to swing to the west towards the loading ramp. What was more troubling was that some of them had swung towards the facility itself. One started to move toward the building, then others followed.

"What the hell is that?" Topeka asked, pointing at the screen.

In the foreground, plant-things were heading to the facility, but she was pointing to the background. Colby bent over to get a closer look. The pod had crushed the plants on the rails into mush, but not all of them. Many, probably those on the edges, had simply been torn apart. As Colby watched, the parts, scattered over the landscape, started to twitch. To his utter amazement, a torn leafy branch pulled itself to what had been a central stalk and hugged it. He couldn't tell for sure with the display's resolution, but it looked like it melded into the stalk.

"Oh, hell, they're reanimating!" Topeka said.

The branch pulled itself and the stalk to the side where another chunk of stalk lay and pulled it in. After a few moments, that second chunk was absorbed into the first.

Colby felt a deep misgiving. If they could reanimate, then that changed the rules of the game. He and Topeka had to do something now. If they waited, they'd be in much deeper shit.

"Get ready," he said, wishing he'd had time to discuss a plan of action with her first.

Even with Marines, men and women who put in immense amount of time training in the deadly arts, there should be operations orders and rehearsals. Topeka, who was evidently quite capable at her work, was still a civilian, and the best he could do with her was to simply say "Get ready?"

He pulled her by the arm to the cases of ANFO grenades. He'd made these to detonate upon impact, so it was simply a matter of throwing them. The flamethrower took a few more minutes to teach her to work it. The air had to be released first, then once the stream of jelly was being shot out, then, and only then, could it be lit off. The flame was a very simple device, the spark caused by touching a naked piece of wire to a tiny fuel cell.

She assured him she had it as there was a crash against the back of the building. The plant soldiers had reached them.

Colby rolled the cylinder forward, and Topeka picked it up with her forks. He ran the ignition wire back to her, then slapped the fuel cell to the vertical strut of the cage. Taking a roll of duct tape, the ubiquitous must-have for any shop for the last millennium, he affixed the wand to one of the forks. She'd have to control the direction of the fire with the lift.

"Remember, don't touch off the ignition—"

". . . until the air is releasing, I know, I know."

Colby slapped the cylinder, then grabbed the lift yoke. It was a standard model, used to lift up to 500 kg. He'd never liked the loss of mobility the leg braces created, but he'd be a lot more mobile than if he was horsing the cylinder on his own.

He picked up his cylinder, locking it into the harness. This left an arm free to hold the wand. Grabbing six grenades, he slipped each one into a separate compartment.

There was a loud crash as the back wall gave in.

"You ready?" he asked Topeka.

"It's go-go time," she shouted, using the pet phrase of Major Mountie, Space Explorer.

He managed not to roll his eyes. He hated that asinine, juvenile series.

"You're not maneuverable enough to stay inside here. Go outside, then move to the left to engage. I'll take care of these," he said, wheeling to face the back of the control room.

She nodded, then drove her little forklift out the door.

Colby readied his wand, then stepped forward to join the battle.

When Colby was a young lieutenant, zombie flicks had been popular, with mindless undead pursuing dwindling numbers of the living. As the plant soldiers pulled themselves through the wall with green leafy arms, he was struck by how close the image looked like old zombies breaking into houses, singularly intent on devouring brains.

He shook his head to clear the vision, then opened up the compressed air. A moment later, the jet caught the flammable jelly, sending it out to splash on the enemy. He thought he saw a few of the plant-things flinch, but before he could contemplate the significance of that, he touched off the jelly. Immediately, a rush of flame reached out, so hot the heat against his face made him flinch.

The plants went up most satisfyingly. Within ten seconds, every one of them was on fire, a few staggering, but most slumped to the floor, rapidly disintegrating under the onslaught.

"Get some!' he shouted, stepping forward to give him a better field of fire to outside the broken wall.

More of the plants walked forward into the flame, and Colby felt a rush of exultation. His flamethrower was working, and the stupid things were helpless before him.

And then there were none in view. He kept the stream going for a moment, but he didn't have an unlimited amount of fuel or compressed air, so he cut off the flow. The floor in front of him, as well as the inner walls near the break, were still on fire, the acrid smoke making his eyes burn.

For a moment, he thought he might have defeated the enemy, but through tearing eyes, he could still see masses of green just out of reach of his flamethrower. He edged to the side to give himself a better angle, and suddenly, the attention of the plants seemed to shift away from him. Almost in unison, the mass started to the right.

Topeka!

He'd told her to take her forklift in that direction, and he knew she was engaging. Taking one of his grenades, he armed and tossed it out through the break in the wall, almost hitting the edge and bouncing it back to his feet, but the grenade landed outside with a satisfying explosion, blowing bits of green into the air. The mass continued to move, though, and Colby knew he couldn't do much from inside the building. He needed broader fields of fire.

"Come on, Duke!" he shouted, wheeling around, pushing against the inertia of his flamethrower.

The dog was nowhere in sight, but he didn't have time to look for her. He almost stumbled out the door, then turned right. With Topeka on the other side of the building, he wanted to hit the mass of plant soldiers from their rear.

It was taking him a bit of effort to deal with the Daihatsu lifter. The 100-kg flamethrower might feel like it weighed 15 or 20 kg, but like the cargo pod, the mass was the mass. That didn't change. Colby had to lean into the turn to horse the thing around the corner of the building, then sprint along the side and to the front. He could see plant soldiers moving as a single unit towards the south and where Topeka would be hitting them. As soon as he was in range, he opened the air, igniting the flames once the slightly pink jelly shot out.

And, of course, he forgot about his momentum. Not only was turning difficult, but so was stopping. He was barely able to nudge his direction to the side in order to avoid the burning jelly and plant-soldiers on the ground as he rushed forward. His unprotected face blistered in the heat.

He forced the pain from his mind as he spun around, swinging his wand to lay down sheets of fire. Ahead of him, near the far side of the building, ropes of flame revealed where Topeka engaged the plants.

There had to be hundreds of the enemy between them, and for a moment, Colby thought the two humans had them trapped, but as he swung his wand to the right, he caught a glimpse of hundreds more of the plant-soldiers peeling off around the launch terminal.

At that moment, it sunk in. He'd assumed that the slower-moving enemy were mindless, automatons like the zombies in the flicks. But that had been a mistake. What he was seeing was tactics, pure and simple. The enemy between Topeka and him were a fixing force while the main body was maneuvering to envelope her. Coming up from behind her, she couldn't fire in two directions at once, and she'd be engulfed.

Never underestimate your enemy, Edson! he reminded himself.

Topeka wouldn't know she was in deep shit, and he was not about to let her be overrun. With his right hand controlling the flames, he tossed each of his remaining grenades in front of him, sending up gouts of plant tissue and green mist.

"I'm coming in for you!" he shouted, trying to get her attention so she didn't crisp him in her battle fury.

He could just see the top of the forklift, but the wall of flame that had been swinging towards him reversed course. Leaning forward, he pushed ahead, gaining speed and momentum, keeping his own flame to Topeka's left. He crashed through a line three deep of the plant soldiers, almost breaking into the clear beside her. One plant had managed to grasp the edge of his lifter, and amazingly, started to bodily pivot Colby around. He could sense he was getting dragged back, and he tried to bring his wand to bear, but the thing was too close, and the flames were shooting over it.

Colby was about to shuck the lifting harness when a string of fire, much depleted from what it should be, splashed the plant, and it recoiled, letting him go.

Topeka had come to his rescue, but in doing so, had opened her back, just as the flanking plant soldiers rounded the launch terminal.

"Behind you!" he shouted, unable to engage with her between the enemy and him.

Topeka's look of jubilation at having saved his ass turned to fear as she saw the enemy converge on her. She swung her wand, but barely a dribble of flame shot out for five meters, well short of the threat. Colby's flamethrower still had a good charge, but either she'd expended much more of her air then he had or he'd just not put as much into hers.

With a sweep to his left, he bolted forward to her, shouting, "I've got your six. Now, back out of here."

She didn't argue, which was a relief. With a curt nod, she put the forklift into reverse. Colby followed, back to her as he sprayed one swipe after the other, trying to slow down the onslaught.

He couldn't keep it up. The plant soldiers moved slower than a human could, but they were fast enough to close the distance with him walking backwards.

"Can't that thing go any faster?" he asked her.

"This is about it," she answered, her voice cracking from the stress.

She tried another shot, but the flame quit after only a second. She was out of either fuel or compressed air.

Colby flamed five of the closest enemy, then looked back. They were about to be cut off, with only a tight seven or eight-meter lane alongside the eastern wall of the building. Then something else caught his eyes. Beyond the attackers, over where the other plants had looked to be somehow merging their bodies, two green figures rose, and his stomach churned. They had to be standing ten meters tall. As he watched a huge leafy hand reached down out of his line of sight, then reappeared with a piece of plant-part. It stuck the part to its side, held it for a moment, then released. The piece of plant was absorbed into the huge body. The other giant rummaged in the remains for additional parts as well. If those two joined the fight, Colby's little flamethrower wasn't going to do him much good.

He didn't try and analyze the situation. He didn't weigh the pros and cons of various courses of action. He made the decision before he really thought through the problem.

"Get out of the lift and run for it!" he shouted in his best voice of command, one that brooked no dissent.

With a smooth movement, he shucked his lift assist, clamping down the wand release and pushing it forward. The stream of flame acted like a tug-bot motor, slowly rotating it back towards him. He didn't try and correct it. Either he was fast enough to make it clear or he wasn't, and hesitating would seal the deal. He bolted after Topeka, watching out of the corner of his eyes as the flame slowly moved to intercept him.

It also incinerated the plant soldiers that were reaching out for him as he sprinted. He expected either the grasp of green strength or the kiss of fire to bring him down, but somehow, with only centimeters to spare, he managed to avoid death. The hair on the back of his head felt as if it'd been singed, but he was in the clear, pelting after a surprisingly quick Topeka.

And then he remembered his remaining grenades.

"Wait!" he shouted, but she wasn't slowing down.

He'd managed to open up some space around him, so he turned to the right and ran down the length of the back wall. Stopping just short of the door, he peeked inside. The front wall and the control room had been destroyed, and he could see movement all the way through the building, but otherwise the room was empty. He darted in, then swept the grenades back into the carrying case.

"Easy, boy. Don't set them off now."

He knew he didn't have time, but he'd be naked without a weapon. Poking his head out of the door, he could see that twenty or thirty of the enemy had cleared the corner of the building. From this side of the building, he didn't see the two giants, but knew they would be coming.

"This way!" Topeka shouted at him. "We've got to lead them the fuck away from here."

She was standing by the ruined shell of Warehouse B, frantically waving her arm for him to join her. He didn't know where she was heading, but anyplace had to be better than where he was.

Marines never liked to retreat. It wasn't in their DNA. But sometimes, discretion was the better part of valor, and with Riordan in the med chamber somewhere in the building, she was right. If the man was going to survive, the two of them had to clear the area. Without any more flames, they had to act the rabbit.

I might as well get their attention, he told himself as he lowered the case and took out one of the grenades.

He arched it in a beautiful throw, landing it right at the leading edge of the oncoming enemy. Colby knew that the plant soldiers were latched onto them and he hadn't needed the grenade, but it sure felt good to see salad being made before he took off to follow Topeka. The plant bastards would follow at their own pace.

Interlude II: Harvest

Telemetry flowed to the Gardener's vessel, chemical signals released by the mature plants resulting from the second wave of spores it had unleashed during the previous dark cycle. The vessel processed them without judgment, collating and compiling information and feeding it to the roots of the Gardener's navigation locker. Information could be a form of nourishment, but these reports soured rather than fueled the Gardener. Despite its earlier suppositions, its unleashed tools had not encountered any Mechanicals. The remnants of their limited visual processing described only a handful of pathetic, right-angled structures, the sort of boxes that Meat created when given the chance. That, and a single massive structure that had somehow launched a pod of its own through the atmosphere and into the surrounding space. The Gardener's own craft had lost track of the thing. One moment it had been clearing the world's exosphere and when scans next swept that location where it should have been, it had vanished. The Gardener spared a few cycles to review the pod's trajectory and extrapolate its location in space, but further scans were fruitless. It couldn't be found anywhere. Strange.

Stranger still, the force it had planted to dismantle those offending structures had failed. A significant portion had expired prematurely, releasing chemo-signatures into the air tallying their demise. Mechanicals would never have bothered engaging vegetation and Meat lacked the sophistication to offer a challenge to such a degree. Strangest of all though was that the remainder of its tools had turned from their task, the destruction of the structure responsible for the now-missing pod. Instead of completing the disassembly, the survivors had abandoned the converging ring formation the Gardener had encoded into their spores and reformed into a ragged line that hurtled across an open plain toward the edge of a forest. Pointless. This planting, even more than the first one, had limited resources of strength and duration. More than half would exhaust themselves before they had crossed even half the distance. Worse still, those that endured and entered the forest would be lost to its sensors, their chemical telemetry absorbed and blocked by the trees above them.

Something had gone wrong. A string of somethings, in fact, and two rounds of purge agents had not resolved the discrepancies. The second planting would not, could not, deviate from their coded tropism without a compelling stimulus. Another something even now led them into the forest, subverting the mindlessness that should have been sufficient to the task at hand.

The Gardner roused itself to fuller wakefulness within its navigation pod. It considered the imperfection of its results. Perhaps it had erred, reacting too directly to the intrusion in its garden. A literal perspective rarely served. After all, its art thrived on the figurative. It opened itself to the memories of past cycles of growth and found a metaphor from its earliest teacher, a memory it had tucked away in ages past for just such a need as it now felt.

Where the branches cannot reach, the roots must dive deeper.

Then too, perhaps not quite so figurative after all. The Gardener released chemical signals to the receptors of its navigation locker. The vessel responded to the commands and slipped from orbit, spiraling soundlessly downward into the atmosphere, targeting the same copse of trees that had captivated the remnant of the second planting. To understand the situation, the Gardener would have to descend to the planet's surface and resolve the matter within the forest itself. Only then could it return to tending the garden it planned for this world.

Part III: Resolution and Threat

"Are they still following?" Topeka asked, her breath coming hard.

"You just keep moving," Colby told her, "And let me worry about them."

Duke yipped with an enthusiasm she'd never displayed before. Apparently fleeing an alien invasion had inspired her. She had rejoined them as they ran through the rubble just ahead of the plants. Together, the three had crossed the open area surrounding the station, pulling farther ahead of their pursuers. That had started to change. Topeka was struggling, now. She'd proven herself to be a hardass during the fight, but too many hours sitting in her control seat had cut into her fitness. Despite having at least 30 years on her, his daily exercise routine had kept him in excellent shape, and he'd barely broken a sweat.

"Can we stop for a minute?" Topeka asked, barely getting the words out as they reached the far treeline, about four klicks from the station.

Colby wanted to keep running, but slowed. He'd lose her otherwise.

"OK, but just for a minute," he said as she came to a stop and bent over, hands on her knees.

Duke ran up to her and licked her face.

Colby looked back along the way they'd come. The mass of smaller plants had actually followed them out of the station complex, away from Riordan in his med chamber. Even with Topeka huffing and puffing, they'd opened up at least a two-klick gap between them and the pursuers. But something had changed. The main body of plants chasing them had thinned out. Those in the front continued in their pursuit, but those towards the rear were barely moving. Some of those had fallen, and through the gaps in the front line, Colby could see them lay prone on the ground. Even as he watched, more of those in the front ranks started to fall back. Colby wondered if the plants had varying degrees of fitness just as the two humans had.

Towards the rear of the pack, the two giants had slowed as well, but remained clearly focused on them. Then, with no warning, one ponderously turned and lumbered back the way it had come, returning to the station. The other one kept oriented towards them for a long 20 seconds. At the risk of anthropomorphizing the things, Colby thought it reluctantly turned to join the other, heedlessly smashing some of its smaller brethren.

But where the small ones were dropping like flies, the giants didn't move as if they were fatigued.

"You doing OK?" he asked Topeka as he watched the giants walk back into the station.

"Yeah. No. Shit, just give me another minute," she said, anger dripping from her voice.

Colby watched her, evaluating her as he had many soldiers over the years. Was her anger at the plants or aimed at herself for not being able to keep up? Probably a bit of both. Anger was usually a liability in a battle, but if he could use it to keep her moving, he would.

"Those bastards . . ." he started, then stopped, looking out over the broken ranks of pursuing plants.

"Those bastards what?"

"Look at that. Some of them, they look like they're decomposing," he said.

It was true. While the closest few plants were still pursuing them, the ones farthest back, the ones that had fallen, were flattening out. Maybe a few had been smashed flat by the retreating giant, but most seemed to be wilting and breaking down. Wisps of green mist rose above the plant corpses before being dissipated by the breeze. Even the nearer plants that were still coming at them didn't look healthy.

"Fuck them," Topeka said, straightening. Still, she looked back, stepping around Colby for a better view. "You're right. They're going straight into compost."

With the chase petering out, Colby didn't see a need to push on, and Topeka could use the break, so he watched what was happening. He wished he had a pair of binos to see better, but even with his naked eyes, he could see more and more of them staggering as the roots they walked on gave way.

But not with the giants. They had made it back to the launcher and tore into it, their leafy arms twisting and tearing the ceramalloy like so much tissue paper. If they could do that, then the launch facility, with Riordan inside, wouldn't stand a chance if they turned their attention to it.

As if on cue, Topeka asked, "How does the house look?"

Colby shifted his gaze. The building in which she'd stashed Riordan was one of the few still standing. But it was only a matter of time. If a pair of plant giants could completely demolish a launch mechanism designed to withstand the stressors associated with payloads at gravity-defying velocities and last a hundred years doing so, he knew they could make short work of any building on the planet. And there was nothing they could do about it.

Topeka had to have come to the same conclusion, but she just stood there, saying nothing.

Colby was a general—a disgraced general, true, but a general nonetheless. Marines didn't earn their stars unless they had that take-charge attitude needed to fight their Marines. He stood there with only a civilian and a dog, but his mind kept churning on how he could turn the three of them into a task force that could defeat the enemy.

No miracle plan popped into his mind.

"I sure wish I knew what was going on everywhere else," Topeka said, as she stared back toward the station.

Colby hit himself in the forehead. The local net had been knocked out and Topeka might be cut off, but he had his military implant. He'd largely forgotten about it after calling Erin. Ralph, the farm AI, was connected to the local repeaters and was now silent with them knocked out, but the implant was connected to the hadron comms ecosystem. It didn't need to rely on planet-based repeaters and could create networks almost out of thin air.

He activated the implant, feeling the familiar surge as it hugged his brain. The implant was downloading terrabytes of information from thousands, if not tens of thousands of sources, from any PA on the planet still transmitting to satellites in orbit. The shared volume of information pouring in threatened to overwhelm him. The key in getting something useful from all that data was knowing how to manage it in usable forms, and Colby had years of practice doing that.

He immediately created a filter to isolate inputs into a series of categories. The first one was for human transmissions, hoping to see if anyone else had survived and was trying to contact others. That folder was empty.

His implant had flagged another folder with a red alert message. This one was for vehicular movement, which might mean someone was trying to come to the station. Colby quickly opened it, but was confused. No surface movement had been identified, but rather something high in the sky.

What the hell is that? It looked to be coming in from outside the planet's atmosphere.

He narrowed his search parameters, and the explanation came into focus. Something was heading to the planet's surface.

"We've got company coming," he told Topeka.

"What do you mean?"

"I mean, something is coming in for a landing, something not in any database. You told me there was a ship in orbit that was the source of the plants we've been fighting. If I had to guess, I'd say the plant boss is coming to take a look at what's happening here."

"How do you know that?" she asked. "The system's down, and my PA ain't working for shit."

"I've still got my implant," he told her, pointing to his temple.

"So? I've got mine, too."

"Uh. . . mine. . . well, it's got a few more capabilities than yours. I'm connected to the hadron ecosystem."

"So, can you order up a navy battleship or something?"

"Not exactly. I already attempted to get us some help, but I sort of got the door slammed in my face."

She let that sink in, then said, "General, you must have fucked up royally. We always wondered why you were here on this shithole in the ass end of the galaxy, and if they won't even talk to you. . ."

Colby ignored the dig and ran a landing trajectory. He wasn't surprised that the ship was going to land nearby. If this was the general calling the shots, or even just some version of an inspector, it would want to be near the troops.

He turned to look back at the plant soldiers again. A few were still advancing, even more slowly than before, but most were down and becoming compost.

Pretty lousy soldiers, if they can't even pursue us, he thought, forgetting for the moment at how easy they'd demolished his farm and the station.

"So, where's this motherfucker landing?" Topeka asked.

"Unless it alters its course, about 800 meters thataway," he answered, pointing deeper into the trees.

Topeka pulled a machete out of her pack and said, "Then I say we go meet this piece of shit and teach it a fucking lesson."

****

"Remember, we're only trying to gather some intel," he told Topeka as they crept forward through the trees.

"You already told me that, like ten times, already, too," Topeka snarled.

If the whitening of her hands around the handle of her machete was any indication, she wanted, no, needed, to kick some ass. And that could be a disaster. Until he knew exactly what they faced, any rash action might screw things up.

Colby understood Topeka's emotional state, however. He was a Marine, and he'd lost friends, leaders, and his troops in combat. No warrior could ever forget that. Topeka had lost her friends as well, and Riordan was back in a med chamber right now, at risk from some giant broccoli. She was angry, and she wanted revenge. It was up to Colby to hold her back until he had a better grasp of the situation.

Behind Topeka, Duke started whining.

"Quiet, girl," he said, kneeling with his hands out to her.

She ignored him, her attention riveted to the front. It was evident that she did not want to go any further.

"Wait here," he told Topeka before grabbing Duke's collar and leading her back 20 meters.

He hadn't thought to bring a leash, and there weren't any handy vines that every hero in any Hollybolly flick seemed to find when they needed a rope. With a sense of resignation, he pulled off his belt, looped it through her collar, and tied it off on a low branch.

"Stay here, girl. And please, don't bark," he said, cradling her head in his hands.

Her brown eyes looked up at him. He wondered what was going on in her little dog mind. She understood something was very wrong, that much was certain. She'd been whining at something, after all. He rubbed her belly for a few moments, and with an almost human sigh, she lay down and rolled onto her back. He kept it up for a full minute, feeling her fur through his fingers, hoping this wouldn't be the last time he'd be doing it. He'd inherited Duke, and she'd grown on him. Him. General Colby Meritt Edson. A dog lover?

"That's enough, girl. I've got to go."

She whumped her tail once on the ground, but didn't bark. With a last pat on her head and a pull to hitch up his pants, he left her there.

"What did you do with her?" Topeka asked as he caught up with her again.

"What? I tied her to a tree so she won't get hurt. Why, what do you think I did?" he asked confused.

"Oh, I don't know. I'm not a soldier," she said, her voice restrained and emotionless.

What the hell does she think I am?

He almost demanded that she come back with him to see Duke for herself, but he shook it off. Up ahead was the enemy. She'd see Duke soon enough.

"OK, let's move up, but slowly. We don't want to be picked up by any pickets."

"Pickets? You mean a fence?"

"No, pickets. Uh. . . sentries. Soldiers sent out to make sure no one like us sneaks up on them."

"Why didn't you just say 'sentries' in the first place," she muttered under her breath.

Colby chose to ignore the comment. She wasn't a Marine, and he wasn't her commander. Still, it took a force of will to turn away.

The thought of pickets gave him pause, though. He wanted to conduct a quick recon, find out what was there, then get back unseen to decide their next course of action. But if there was a picket, then they might be spotted, and they'd have to defend themselves—and they didn't have all that much with which to do it. Sure, they still had a few grenades, but no direct fire weapons.

But, relatively speaking, rifles and beamers were only the more recent weapons man had ever used.

He held his hand out for the machete, which Topeka reluctantly gave him. They were in a fir forest, a common terraforming tree. A fast growing, renewable resource with a million and one uses. Firs were not the best for what he had in mind, but not the worst by any stretch of the imagination, either.

With Topeka looking at him as if he were crazy, he selected four young trees, each about three-to-four meters tall. A few whacks with the machete, and they were down. Working quickly, he stripped the branches, leaving the central shaft bare. He hefted one to his shoulder and balanced it for a moment. Satisfied with the feel, he laid them down and cut each shaft to about two meters in length.

He was so caught up in what he was doing, it was a few moments before he remembered that Topeka was much smaller than him. Looking up at her, he mentally measured her height and arm length, then lopped off another half-meter from two of them. A few more chops with the extremely sharp machete, and he had pointed tips.

If I had more time, I'd fire harden the tips.

If I had more time, I'd fit a metal head on each of these, he admonished himself. *Or requisition a meson beamer. Hell, might as well go for broke and call in a Navy battleship.*

These were not the best spears ever made, but they could use them in a pinch, not waiting for a grenade to go off. There were too many unknowns ahead of them, and a few seconds might make the difference between life and death.

There was one more easy thing he could do to improve the crude spears' effectiveness. Colby searched the detritus on the ground until he found a piece of wood that would serve. With a few more cuts of his trusty machete, he fashioned an axolotl. Colby had employed them many times during Escape and Evasion exercises, and they were surprisingly easy to use.

"Are you done farting around, General?" Topeka asked.

"Have you ever used one of these?"

"Used one? I don't know what the hell it is."

Colby frowned. He'd expected her to at least know that much.

"These are your spears," he said, handing her the two shorter ones.

"I'll take the machete," she said, hand out. "And I've got the grenades you gave me."

He gave it back, but added, "The grenades have about a ten-meter ECR. . . uh, that means, Effective Casualty Radius. Any nearer, they'll get you, too. And you'll have to close in with one of them to use your machete."

"Close with who? We don't even know what we're facing."

"That's my point," said Colby, shaking one of the spears to bring her attention back to them. "With these babies you can hold them off. Given the right opportunity you can even throw them."

"Throw them? You only made two for me."

"Right, which is why you should avoid doing that, if you can help it. But if you do have to throw, this axolotl will put more power into it. Here, try it."

He showed Topeka how to use the axolotl and had her practice half-a-dozen throws at the trunk of a large tree ten meters away. She missed each time and was getting frustrated.

"OK, don't throw if you have to. Just stab anything that comes close."

"Stupid *axo-tot-o*," she muttered and she slipped it through her belt.

"OK, then, I think we're ready. Let's go find our spaceship."

They didn't have to advance far. Within 50 meters, they reached a small opening in the trees. Smack-dab in the middle of the opening was what looked like nothing more than a 20-meter long, mottled greenish-black seed pod. There was no doubt, however, that this was a ship, a huge, space-faring zucchini.

Topeka stopped for a moment, then reached for one of her grenades, taking a step forward before Colby grabbed her and pulled her to the ground.

"We're here to observe, now," he hissed through clenched teeth.

She glared daggers at him, but nodded.

Around the spaceship, several small plants moved about, poking rope-like tendrils into the ground and holding feathery-looking branches into the air. Colby didn't need anyone to tell him that they were taking measurements.

"They're taking measurements," Topeka said anyway.

Colby shushed her.

The side of the ship split open with a one-meter fissure, and a squat plant trundled out. The front elongated into a flat blade, which it used to scoop up some soil before turning back and reentering the ship. The opening sealed shut with nary a sign it had even existed.

"What now?" Topeka asked.

"Now we wait and observe."

He could feel Topeka's frustration, but he wasn't going to rush things. Too much depended on them not going half-cocked.

Sun Tzu had dictated that a soldier had to know his enemy, and there were just too many things that he didn't understand about these plant things. They didn't act like any human enemy he'd known.

First, they hadn't initially attacked him. Their offensive had been aimed at his crops. They'd only moved to him when he'd tried to intervene. That made no sense. Why attack stationary crops when a mobile human, who had the ability to take action, was left alone. The conclusion he'd reached was that the crops themselves were the focus of the mission. They'd attacked him when he tried to interfere with that.

Even at the station, they were focused on the facilities, not the people. He had to wonder, if no one had opposed the plants, would they have still attacked? Would all those people, with their farms destroyed around them, still be alive?

Colby let the hours pass, and as the morning turned to afternoon, there still wasn't any action around the ship to reflect a military operation of conquest. It looked more like a science expedition than anything else. During his military career, he'd seen more than a few boffins in action, overly concerned with taking samples and spinning hypotheses and beyond clueless when it came to strategy and tactics.

The plants had killed people, true. But the more he watched, the more this didn't feel like a war of conquest. Just what it was, he didn't know yet.

All he could do was to observe and hope things became clearer.

****

Late afternoon, and Colby was no closer to an answer. He didn't even know what was in the ship. Nothing over a meter tall had emerged.

Beside him, Topeka had gone beyond antsy and advanced all the way to agitated. If they didn't do something soon, he knew she would explode. But it wasn't clear what, if anything, they could do. They had his grenades, but even if that was the right course of action to take, Colby doubted they held sufficient power to disable the ship. He'd taken retinal-shots of everything in the clearing, and had them queued up for his implant to send to headquarters. But, given his last reception, he knew he needed more.

Like one of them to bring back, alive and whole and not broken down into compost. Which meant *not* waiting around for HQ to send a ship, but bringing the thing directly to them.

Of course, that supposed he had a ship fueled and sitting on the apron, ready to go. Which he didn't. Yes, there might be some fuel stored back at the station, but the only ships on Vasquez were sub-orbital continent hoppers, and if his growing suspicions were right, none of those would have survived the plants' attack any more than his farm had.

While he mourned the lack of a vessel, another fissure opened on the ship in the clearing. This one a little bigger than the others, but otherwise the same. He watched as a slender plant emerged, a woodier variation than any he'd seen before. It had squeezed out of the fissure and then unfolded and unfolded again to a full two meters in height. Colby wondered if it was the ship's operator, but it went to the far side of the clearing and extended a proboscis of sorts and bored into the tree.

Just another lab tech.

"Fuck this shit, I'm going in," Topeka said from beside him.

She jumped to her feet. Colby lunged for her as she bolted, fingers brushing the heel of her boots as she darted across the open area.

It was only then that he saw the last opening had not closed, and he knew that was Topeka's target. He jumped up and chased her, one hand holding up his pants, the other holding a spear. Colby knew he'd be too late. He almost hoped that the two plants between her and the ship would interfere—not hurt her, just delay her down enough for him to catch her, but they ignored her.

Topeka didn't even slow down. Machete in hand, she dove into the opening. Her feet were visible for a moment, then with a kick, they disappeared just as Colby reached the ship.

He hesitated a moment, running through his options. For all he knew, the ship's atmosphere could be poisonous to human life. And what internal or automatic defenses did it possess, ready to spring into action at the first sign of an intruder. And they had defenses. Just touching one of the smaller plants when they'd first arrived at his farm had caused him pain. Topeka's rash action could already have killed her.

But he really had no choice. He had to follow. Taking a big breath of air and leading with a spear still in his hand, he pushed his head and shoulders through the opening. It was tight, very tight, and the walls themselves seemed to push him back. With a grunt, he set his feet, still outside, and pushed, gaining some ground. His legs churned, toes tearing up the dirt, as centimeter by centimeter, he gained ground. His shoulders, then his arms, made it past, and he grabbed at the floor of the entrance, trying to pull himself forward.

He couldn't hold his breath any longer, and he let it out with a gasp, followed by a desperate inhalation. He didn't die. He could breathe. The air smelled funky, a rich, loamy scent that was somehow undercut with the tang of ozone, but he wasn't suffocating or choking out his life. His lungs weren't burning.

The walls of the opening remained tight on him, and as he pushed and pulled himself forward, his pants began slipping. With his arms inside, he couldn't do much about that, so he ignored them.

It took a few more moments of struggle, but he finally made it into the ship—sans pants. It had been like crawling back up the birth canal. The thought made him shudder as he looked around to get his bearings, spear at the ready.

No plant soldiers rushed to attack. There was nothing except for a featureless tunnel, a meter-and-a-half high. Crouched over, Colby crept forward to the end, about four or five meters away. The floor gave way slightly under his feet, which only raised his anxiety.

The tunnel ended in a gate of some sort. He couldn't see any controls, but Topeka had to have gone this way, so holding the spear out, he pushed himself through.

Any lingering doubts vanished. He was in a ship of some sort. It looked nothing like any Navy ship he'd seen, but there was enough organization and instrumentation to register in his mind as something recognizable. Some of the Hollybolly scifi flicks he'd watched had ship bridges far more outlandish.

He spared only a second to let that thought sink in before his attention locked onto Topeka. She stood in the middle of the compartment, machete raised. And on the other side of her was what had to be the general/captain/big boss/whatever of the ship.

It was a plant, but not like any that Colby had seen before. A meter and a quarter tall, it was rounded and symmetrical, having no discernible front or back. It resembled a torpedo more than a man, if someone had painted that torpedo a slick, greenish black and festooned it with dozens of thick, ropey tendrils that began a fifth of the way from the top, just beneath a slight narrowing of its core, a neck of sorts, beneath a rounded pointed "head." The tendrils continued in irregular groupings on down until the ends of the lowest of them pooled out onto the floor around it.

It half stood, half leaned against a depression in the wall where some of its tendrils had reached out and connected to the ship itself, piercing or plugging in, at what on a short human might have corresponded to knee- and waist- and elbow-height. Another grouping at the highest point had splayed out on the side facing Topeka, lining up vertically, side by side. It took Colby a moment before he realized what it looked like— like a man raising both hands in a warding gesture, almost pleading, having backed itself away as far as it could.

It wasn't just fearful, it was scared. Scared for its life.

This wasn't a general, and if it was the ship's captain it was probably only by virtue of being the only sapient being on the ship at all. It hadn't come to fight, that much was clear. Just as Colby could see that Topeka couldn't care less.

"Stop, Topeka! We need to capture it!" he shouted.

She turned to him, and the honest pain on her face underscored her words as she said simply, "It killed my friends."

Before she could turn back, the plant opened a sphincter and let out a puff of air that blew

Topeka's hair about, and stopped her in her tracks. Colby froze, expecting to see her collapse or start melting like in the horror flicks, but she slowly wiped her forehead and looked at her arm.

"Is that the best you've got? A fart?" she asked, taking another step forward.

"Wait, what's that?" Colby said, grabbing her by the shoulder and pointing to the small beads that had been smeared around her face when she wiped it.

"Don't know," she said, wiping the back of one hand across the opposing sleeve. "They felt like a sandstorm for a moment when it shot them at me, but they're nothing now."

"They could be poisonous."

"All the more reason to end this shit now!"

She pulled out of his grasp and stepped forward, machete raised.

The plant-thing shambled to its left with surprising speed, eager to put some distance between the small woman and itself. Colby took the opportunity to dart forward, stepping between the two. That probably wasn't the smartest thing to do, what with a creature of unknown capabilities on one side and a crazed woman armed with a machete and hungry for revenge on the other, but he needed to capture the plant, not kill it.

At least the plant wasn't shooting him with some kind of death ray. In fact, it still looked like it was trying to escape from the two of them. Keeping in front of Topeka, he advanced on the thing. Colby had been the Combined Military *Atarashi Karate* champion back when he was a lieutenant. He'd kept up his fitness, but he wasn't sure his training translated into subduing an alien plant.

As if he was still in competition, his body memory pulled him into his *kokutsu-dachi* stance, body back over his rear leg, left foot thrust forward as he tried to analyze his opponent.

How do you analyze a giant artichoke?

He couldn't just stand there. That would invite attack or let Topeka get around him. He stepped forward to deliver a *mai geri* kick. . . and the plant shot a tendril at one of the little helper plants along the bulkhead and threw it at him, smacking Colby in the face before he could block it.

There wasn't much power behind the throw, but it stung, like getting slapped in the face. The plant's many tendrils started picking up everything in its reach and throwing them. Colby ducked several more, and from the curses from behind him, he knew some were connecting with Topeka.

"Get out of my way!" she yelled as she pushed past him just as a small, ropy plant hit her square in the face, making her stumble.

She fell into the wall with a thud and collapsed, the machete clattering across the deck and making him jump to avoid the razor-sharp blade.

Colby couldn't tell if she was seriously hurt, but the berserker in him rose to take over in a wave of anger. Forgetting all the niceties of *Atarashi Karate*, he let out a bellow and charged. The plant threw two more small plants, each missing as it panicked, then tried to hit him with another blast of rancid, fetid air.

None of that fazed Colby as he slammed into the plant, knocking it to the ground. He tried to grab anything he could to control it, but it was immensely strong as it struggled to get away. He got both arms around one of the stalks and pulled back with his entire body, arms, legs, and back straining, as he tried to rip it off of the thing.

The result wasn't what he'd expected. Instead of tearing the plant apart, it made an ear-shattering squeal, then went still. Colby didn't know if he'd killed it, if it was surrendering, or if it was trying to trick him. He held on for a few more moments as the plant quivered beneath him. Hesitantly, he started to ease up.

The plant remained still, so he let go and sat back. As soon as it was released, the plant started to inch away, and Colby reached back up to grab the stalk again. It froze immediately.

It knows if it moves, I'll tear it apart. That proves it's intelligent, he told himself.

"Hell, of course it's intelligent. It's got a freaking spaceship!" he said aloud. "Use your brain, Edson!"

He had to secure the plant, and if he'd still had his belt, that would be a start. He might even have made do with the legs from his pants, but he was down to his BVDs. He looked back to Topeka for a moment, who was starting to stir. She had a belt, but he wasn't going to start disrobing a half-conscious woman.

There wasn't much else he could see. The interior of the ship was not cluttered like a tramp steamer. There wasn't a handy coil of monofilament lying around. The only long ropy thing was the. . .

Colby reached up one more time as if to grab the plants stalk, and it shrunk away from him, but didn't try to escape. He stood up and grabbed one of the small plants the alien had thrown at them. The tendril-like arms were rubbery, not like real rope, but it would have to do. Pulling the first tendril to its full length, he wrapped it around two of the big plant's stalks, bringing them together.

With a quick clove hitch, he secured it shut. The small plant had five such tendrils. He was tempted to just pull them free and use them as individual sections of rope, but he didn't know how his prisoner would react. Better to keep it calm. There were three more of the ropy plants he could see: a total of 19 more arms.

He didn't need them all. After ten, it was obvious that their adversary was trussed up like a pig ready for the spit. It wasn't going anywhere.

Colby looked down at the big plant, breathing heavily. They'd done it. They'd captured the thing. This was the proof he needed to convince the government of the threat, and unlike the spores and the plants it had unleashed on Vasquez, his gut told him this thing wasn't going to decompose on him any time soon.

"Can you understand me?" he asked.

The thing didn't respond, not that he'd expected it to. It would have been asking too much for it to have responded with any variation on the "Take me to your leader" trope in crisp Standard.

But a spaceship, even one operated by a sapient plant, was too complex a piece of equipment to operate by hand. It had to possess computers, or plant analogs to computers, and Colby's implant was one of the most advanced pieces of technology ever developed. He didn't need to be able to talk directly to his vegetable adversary, not if his implant could communicate with the ship, then he could use that to query the plant. And he needed answers. The battle was over and done. The casualties had yet to be tallied and assessing the full extent of the damage and its impact on provisioning the war effort would take time. But all of that was secondary. He had to find out why it had attacked the planet.

Colby reached out to his implant, opening its access paths to their broadest capacity and giving it a free hand to scan up and down the electromagnetic, mass, energy, and discrete spectra for anything that might carry a signal or provide a path way to communication. "Can you interface with this ship?" There was a delay of almost six seconds, which was centuries in implant time.

"Yes, in a fashion. I have made contact, but there is yet to be a full interface."

"Keep trying. I want to be able to talk with this thing."

He turned to Topeka, who was only now sitting up. He hurried over to her, helping her to her feet, and asked, "Are you OK? You hit the wall pretty hard."

"Yeah, I'm fine," she asked. "Is it dead?"

"No, I've got it restrained. It's missing a few parts, and its hurt, but it isn't dead."

She shook off his arm and stood on her own. She'd dropped the machete when she'd been flung across the tiny space, and now with real deliberation she walked over to it and picked it up again. Her eyes blazed with anger as she hefted it.

"Topeka," he said, not liking her look. "Remember, we need to get it back to the government. They need to interrogate it."

"Interrogate it my ass. That thing killed Sestus."

"No!" Colby shouted, but in letting her retrieve the blade he'd mistakenly allowed her to get between him and the plant.

With a lunge, Topeka closed the distance with the plant. She gripped the machete with both hands, and with one quick stroke its molecularly-sharp edge cut right through what Colby assumed served as the thing's neck. The head plopped onto the floor with a sound like a crashing watermelon as the rest of the body slumped in the restraints he'd fashioned.

"What they hell have you done?" Colby cried as he rushed forward.

He pulled the machete from her unresisting fingers, too little, too late.

"Revenge, General. I got my revenge."

****

"Are you sure you want to do this?" Colby asked.

"Yeah. I've got to see to Riordan."

They stood outside the ship. Topeka had squirmed back through the way they'd come and Colby had followed more slowly. She'd left his pants for him and went off to retrieve Duke while he pulled himself through the fissure and reclothed himself. Duke had come running into the clearing, tail wagging with more enthusiasm than she'd ever managed for breakfast before. Topeka handed him his belt.

"What if the giants breached the part of the station where you stashed him? We don't even know if they're still out there."

"Yeah, so? You think my odds are worse than your plan to somehow take this alien piece of shit through the wormhole?"

She had a point. His implant was still going through trillions of queries and responses with the plant's ship, trying to create a communications matrix. Colby was confident that he could lift the ship off the planet's surface now, but navigating it through a wormhole in order to make his way back to HQ and present the proof of his claims was in no way a done deal. Even if he could aim it at the wormhole, the plant's ship might not be able to withstand the trip through. His implant had yet to identify anything that might be the vegetable analog of an escape pod. If the ship's integrity failed, he'd die in the nonspace between. No one would ever find his body. He'd uplinked as much data as he could, but with headquarters alerted to his implant's previous hack, he had no doubt that the vice minister had since erected barriers to its efforts. His reports might be queued up in a buffer that no one would ever access. If they did get through, Greenstein might not believe him. The man had made a career from lying on paper and that's how he'd see Colby's outlandish claims of a planetary attack by an intelligent, alien vegetable. No, Colby needed to present the ship and the body of the plant back to the government. He might have been cashiered, but he still knew enough people who would act upon what was right in front of their faces.

He had assumed that Topeka would come with him, but with the plant-thing dead, she seemed to have lost her fire. It had all happened so fast. A day ago she'd been fighting for her life, and when she'd survived, healthy and whole, alone among everyone she knew, she'd been consumed by the need for revenge. After she killed the alien plant-creature, nothing remained to drive her, and the enormity of her losses sunk in. Now, she only wanted to get back to Riordan and begin the process of rebuilding.

There was absolutely nothing she could do for her friend. He had to remain in the med chamber if he was ever going to survive. Colby doubted she could do much in the way of rebuilding. Clean up some of the debris, assemble some solar cells to keep the power going to Riordan's chamber, maybe bring a few of the systems back online, but little more. The launch rails could not be repaired without outside help. But the scheduled shipments had stopped coming, and headquarters would send someone through to investigate, with or without Colby's reports. Still, he understood to some degree her desire to stay busy on the planet, to work at righting some of the wrongs.

Colby's own situation was different. He'd been exiled to the planet, so he had no attachment at all. Sure, he might die trying to get the ship and dead alien back, but he'd faced death in battle countless times before. This would be no different.

"Well, good luck," Colby said, suddenly feeling awkward.

She had driven him crazy, and he was still pissed that she'd killed the plant, but she'd been a good wingman. As good as any Marine he'd served with.

"OK, you too," she said, turning away before she wheeled around and rushed Colby, almost crushing him in a hug.

Colby didn't quite know what to do, but of their own accord, his arms enfolded around her, taking her in.

"And come back for me, General, or I'll come find you and kick your ass," she whispered into his chest.

"I'm sure you would, Topeka. Don't worry, though. We'll get you and Riordan off this mudball."

They held each other for a moment longer before Topeka shifted her hands to his chest and pushed away.

"OK, now, let me get out of here before you destroy the whole forest trying to take off in this thing." Without another look backward she walked out of the clearing.

Colby turned, and with a command to his implant, caused the ship to reluctantly widen the opening that he'd already begun thinking of as the airlock entry.

"C'mon, Duke, inside." For once, the dog did as she was told and clambered into the ship. Colby followed, the entry shaft already dwindling and shoving him forward in a manner all too reminiscent of peristalsis. He strode down the corridor to the spot where he'd encountered the plant creature, the spot that his implant assured him was the nexus of all of the ship's command functions. There was no command chair as humans had, just a rounded depression in the wall, a shallow alcove of sorts. He leaned his back into it and smiled as Duke settled herself on top of his feet.

"Are you ready?" he queried his implant.

"Waiting your command."

"How about you, Duke? You ready?" he asked, reaching down to pat her head.

She whomped her tail on the floor. Whatever else had happened over the last couple of days, he and the dog had finally bonded. For a brief moment, he'd thought about sending her back with Topeka, but he knew that wasn't really an option. She wouldn't have gone, not now, probably not ever.

And truth be told, he was damned happy to have her with him.

"OK, then, let's punch out of this one-horse planet."

He gave the command to his implant, and slowly, the alien spacecraft rose into the sky.

END OF BOOK ONE

Thank you for reading *Invasion*. We hope you enjoyed it. Book 2, *Scorched Earth*, as Colby and Duke continue their fight against the Gardener, will be out soon. We welcome your review of our novella on Amazon or any other website.

SEEDS OF WAR
Invasion
Scorched Earth
Book 3 (Coming Soon).

Other Books by Lawrence M. Schoen

If you would like updates on Lawrence's new books releases, news, or special offers, please consider signing up for his mailing list. Your email will not be sold, rented, or in any other way disseminated. If you are interested, please sign up at the link below:

http://eepurl.com/c7257X

Barsk

Barsk: The Elephants' Graveyard
The Moons of Barsk

The Amazing Conroy
Buffalito Buffet
Calendrical Regression
Barry's Deal

Buffalito Destiny
Trial of the Century
Buffalito Contingency

Selected Short Stories
A Fool's Death
Bidding the Walrus
Pidgin
Mars Needs Baby Seals
The Game of Leaf and Smile
The Moment
Thinking
The Wrestler and the Spear Fisher

Books Edited/Published by Lawrence M. Schoen

Alembical
Alembical 2
Alembical 3
Cats in Space - Elektra Hammond (ed)
Cucurbital 2
Cucurbital 3
Eyes Like Sky and Coal and Moonligh - Cat Rambo
Rejiggering The Thingamajig And Other Stories - Eric James Stone
The Wizard of Macatawa and Other Stories - Tom Doyle

Other Books by Jonathan Brazee

If you would like updates on Jonathan's new books releases, news, or special offers, please consider signing up for his mailing list. Your email will not be sold, rented, or in any other way disseminated. If you are interested, please sign up at the link below:

http://eepurl.com/bnFSHH

The United Federation Marine Corps

Recruit
Sergeant
Lieutenant
Captain
Major
Lieutenant Colonel
Colonel
Commandant

Rebel
(Set in the UFMC universe.)

Behind Enemy Lines
(A UFMC Prequel)

The Accidental War (A Ryck Lysander Short Story Published in *BOB's Bar: Tales from the Multiverse*)

The United Federation Marine Corps' Lysander Twins

Legacy Marines
Esther's Story: Recon Marine
Noah's Story: Marine Tanker
Esther's Story: Special Duty
Blood United

Coda

Women of the United Federation Marine Corps

Gladiator
Sniper
Corpsman

High Value Target (A Gracie Medicine Crow Short Story)
BOLO Mission (A Gracie Medicine Crow Short Story)
Weaponized Math (A Gracie Medicine Crow Novelette, First published in *The Expanding Universe 3*)

The United Federation Marine Corps' Grub Wars
Alliance
The Price of Honor
Division of Power

The Navy of Humankind: Wasp Squadron
Fire Ant
Crystals

Ghost Marines
Integration

The Return of the Marines Trilogy
The Few
The Proud
The Marines

The Al Anbar Chronicles: First Marine Expeditionary Force--Iraq
Prisoner of Fallujah
Combat Corpsman
Sniper

Werewolf of Marines

Werewolf of Marines: Semper Lycanus
Werewolf of Marines: Patria Lycanus
Werewolf of Marines: Pax Lycanus

To the Shores of Tripoli

Wererat

Darwin's Quest: The Search for the Ultimate
Survivor

Assorted Short Stories

Venus: A Paleolithic Short Story
Secession
Duty
Semper Fidelis

Non-Fiction

Exercise for a Longer Life

Author Website
http://www.jonathanbrazee.com